The Streets Bleed Murder 2

Jerry Jackson

Lock Down Publications
Presents
The Streets Bleed Murder 2
A Novel by *Jerry Jackson*

Lock Down Publications
P.O. Box 1482
Pine Lake, Ga 30072-1482

Visit our website at www.lockdownpublications.com

Copyright 2015 by Jerry Jackson The Streets Bleed Murder 2

First Edition October 2015
Printed in the United States of America

This is a work of fiction. Names, characters, places, and incidents either are products of the author's imagination or are used fictitiously. Any similarity to actual events or locales or persons, living or dead, is entirely coincidental.

Lock Down Publications
Facebook: Author Jerry Jackson
Like our page on Facebook: Lock Down Publications @
www.facebook.com/lockdownpublications.ldp
Cover design and layout by: **Dynasty's Cover Me**
Book interior design by: **Shawn Walker**
Edited by: **Lauren Burton**

Dedications

Forever and always, **Jada** and **Kahla**

First it goes to God and then to my family, my friends, my team!

LDP we in da building. Silent money, we on the rise!

Ca$h, I appreciate the opportunity. **Coffee**, thank you, Queen!!! **Coffee** and **Reds Johnson**, thanks for not only being a label mate but a push toward motivation, toward a dream come true. A special thanks to my editor, **Lauren Burton**, and my cover designer, **Dynasty's Cover Me**, thanks two times!!!

Silent money Swole. Shawty, take the game over. Bruh, you got your chance!!! Shout out to my brothers!!!! Y'all niggas know who you are and a great big salute to my lil nigga, Kashtro for being the reason behind my drive. Shawty, you supa dupa solid and I thank God for you, my nigga!! Big Bank, I see you, shawty. I love you, fooly. We been doing this shit ten years almost. My guy and you never changed. East side, I see you, shawty. Billy Tay, I'm fuckin' wit cha bruh and my barber, Cris crazy ass, I see you foo. Lol. Yeah, to the big homie, 'Wewe' a 5ᵗʰ ward champ, you told me I was fi, bruh, and I believed you. Big shout out to the city of ATLANTA and the GA niggas in every prison!!! Always remember to keep your swagg city shit A town over everything. They say we slick. I just say this how we rock.

Great love goes to those that love me. Good love to those who hate. I understand you don't understand me and hey that's cool but here's a few things I'm not: PUSSY? Fuck no! Lame? Nawl, Sucka? Nope. I do not go out bad. I'm most definitely not gay. I only fuck with real

4

niggas and gunners. We don't fold under no pressure and we don't snitch it is what it is.

To all my family, I love y'all, you know that. To all my friends, I know y'all knew I would make something pop, huh? Y'all gon' see me on TV. Lol. Know that I said it first and I'ma show out when I show up. To my father, I love you, my nigga. We not done, trust me. Its many good days to come, old man. Zanny, I love you!!! Oh and Avery and Alli at all times its love, just know dat!!

Jerry Jackson

Chapter 1

Big Geno

"Make the call and get Boss Man on the phone." Big Geno spoke to his partner Max, who was another big dude, but not as big as Geno's six-foot, nine-inch frame, his body built from pure muscle and filled with tattoos. He was a killer by nature, a hustler by heart, while Max did as told. Geno looked down at Gangsta's crumpled-up body sprawled out on his back, face bloody from the gash on his forehead from the blow he took from the gun. Geno walked over to the box containing the money and drugs Gangsta brought along with him. *Job well done,* Big Geno thought to himself as he smiled at what he saw. Moments later Max walked over to join him, then passed him the phone. Geno took a look at it to make sure the call went through.

"Everything good, boss. I got the money and he knocked out cold, so what's next?" Geno asked when he got on the phone with his boss

"Ok, kill everything moving and bring me my money," Boss Man replied, and the phone went dead in his ear. Geno looked to Max and spoke while smiling.

"Everybody dies."

Max smiled when Geno spoke those words.

"So we kill him." Max pulled out his gun and chambered a bullet. He aimed at Gangsta's face, about to pull the trigger, but Geno's voice stopped him.

"Hold up. Go get Merlin and dem hos so we can kill all of them at once. It's a family thing, you know." Geno laughed at his own joke, and Max joined in. Merlin was their driver, and he had Ne-Ne and her sister waiting on their call to either let them go or kill them.

"Ok, cool." Max ran off into the woods, through the back of the cemetery to the houses on the other side where Merlin was parked, waiting on them with the captives.

Geno looked down at Gangsta once again. "Should have got with the team, homie." Geno then reached into his pocket for a cigarette. Proudly lighting it up, he was happy how things were going right then, happy he got the chance to prove to Bam that he was capable of being the right-hand man he'd waited so long to become. Big Geno was head of security to Bam and had been down with him since New York when Bam had first taken over the game with a vicious kingpin named Lucky. Geno worked his way from being a block kid to being Bam's driver for a couple years until one day an attempt was made on Bam's life and Geno saw what was happening and saved him. Geno was then promoted to security and moved up in the ranks. Now, ten years later and so much money made, so many bodies piled up, and he still was down with Bam and was forever loyal.

"Atlanta is ours. Once the Feds clear out, we moving in for the kill," Bam told him one day. Returning from a trip to Miami, Bam had played everyone and gave them up to the Feds, sweeping Atlanta from the biggest to the smallest drug dealers, totaling up thirty-three arrests. Seventy percent would get convicted. Geno had not liked the move, but Bam made it clear to him by saying, "It's either them doing thirty or me and you."

A couple months before the sweep, Bam and Zay got popped in DC with drugs and cash. Bam freed Zay, and days later he resurfaced on the scene. Geno dared not question his boss man. Even though he was not feeling the snitching shit, he rode with him because Bam was smart and was all about the money. Geno had better ideas on how to get money in the streets, but Bam wanted his way or no way — one of the same reasons he and Lucky didn't rock no more.

Lucky had so much love for Bam that he kicked him out of New York rather than killing him. They both just parted ways because Bam didn't want to listen, wanted to always speak, and he was only a right-hand man to Lucky, who ran New York's drug trade with an iron fist. Geno knew it was Bam's plan to take over the drug trade and mimic Lucky's success, but do it his way, and Geno had plans of his owns. Like plans to be Bam's right-hand man. Geno noticed the truck turn into the cemetery and kill the lights as it crept towards the back. Geno held up his hands for Merlin to stop the truck. He and Max climbed out. Merlin was a fat, short guy who was known for his diving skills and his murder game. Max was just a killer by heart.

"Let's get this shit over with," Merlin said. He snatched open the door, pulled Ne-Ne out, and roughly pushed her to the ground. She was cuffed and her ankles were held by duct tape, so she could not break her fall and had to endure the pain. Erica was next. Her face was bruised from the beating Merlin and Max put on her leaving the house. Merlin roughly tossed her out of the truck also, watching her hit the ground, then he pulled out the lil' kid and sat him on the ground.

Big Geno walked over to Ne-Ne with a knife clutched in his fist. He cut through the duct tape to release Ne-Ne's legs, who started kicking and twisting, but her small frame was no match for the 300-pound Geno. He put one of his massive hands around her throat and applied pressure before saying, "Bitch, all the kicking in the world won't stop this show, so you might as well chill the fuck out before I bust up that pretty lil' face of yours. Now, I'm about to cuff you from the front, 'cause I know you uncomfortable, but try anything stupid and you die right then, no questions asked."

Big Geno swiftly put the cuffs on Ne-Ne, then pushed her back down to the ground. He got down with her with lust written all over his face. He had wanted Ne-Ne since laying eyes on her. When they first followed her to her house, he fell in love with her swag and how she carried herself. Geno knew if it came down to killing her, he would first sample the pussy. He wanted her bad, plain and simple. Big Geno kissed the side of Ne-Ne's face, then turned toward Max.

"Cuff that nigga up. I want him woke when I fuck his bitch," Geno ordered his partna. Max walked over to Gangsta, took Gangsta's left hand, and placed a cuff on it. Then he roughly turned him over face-first. Gangsta's free hand was caught up under him.

Ne-Ne was trying to scream through the tape, but failed miserably, so she did what was best: she fought for her life and quickly got slapped.

"Bitch!" Just as Big Geno slapped blood out of her mouth, he heard gunshots.

Boom. Boom. Boom.

He looked over his shoulder just in time to see Max's body fly back, his arms flying wildly as he tumbled. Gangsta was rolling over.

"Shit!" Big Geno said while running for cover behind a large tombstone. Gangsta shot at him, but missed as the bullets tore through the concrete.

***

Gangsta

"Fuck," said Gangsta when he missed the bigger dude. His vision was a blur and his head was killing him. Blood continued to fall from the big gash in his forehead, making it even harder for him to see, though he still tried. All Gangsta knew was that his family depended on him, and he would defend them with his life. He swept the gun around until he saw his son being held by the short, fat guy with a gun pressed to Junior's head. Gangsta stopped everything — the situation had changed that quickly. He wouldn't try big guy, 'cause this wasn't a movie. It was real life. It was his son's life on the line. Blood continued to drip into his eyes. Gangsta had the gun trained on the dude, or at least that's what he thought.

"Drop the gun or he—"

The fat guy could not finish his statement because Ne-Ne jumped to her feet and ran toward him in an effort to save her son, as any mother would do who loved their child, but it was a mistake that cost her. Gangsta did not see the big dude come from behind the tombstone until it was too late. He aimed and shot Ne-Ne two times, sending her crashing face-first into the ground.

And that's when all hell broke loose. Gangsta instantly went into a rage and turned toward the big guy. They both aimed and shot at the same time. Gangsta got hit twice in the chest while the big dude caught one in the face and the other one missed. The pain was so excruciating and breathtaking that Gangsta felt like he was dying, but then he heard another gunshot that quickly got his attention. Gangsta got up to find the fat guy making a break for the truck. Gangsta struggled to a kneeling position, took aim, and let off three shots.

Boom. Boom. Boom.

He missed all three times. His ribs felt broken and he could hardly see. The fat guy was running and shooting over his shoulder. Gangsta, who was in a blind rage, didn't duck or try to dodge the bullets aimed at him. He was determined not to let this nigga get away. The fat guy jumped inside the truck as Gangsta aimed and ran up, the truck roared to life and started to reverse out of the cemetery, but Gangsta wasn't having it as he continued to run up, shooting.

Boom, boom, boom, boom, boom, boom, boom, boom.

Gangsta shot the lights, the grill, the hood, and finally the windshield, and then the fat guy wrecked before making it out of the graveyard. Gangsta wanted to make sure he was dead. He ran over to look inside, and indeed the fat guy was dead. Police sirens could be heard in the distance, and people in Hollywood Court Apartments came out to be nosey.

Gangsta ran over to his family. Ne-Ne was still, face flat in the dirt. Gangsta went to his son, who wasn't moving, his silhouette laid out in the graveyard grass. Gangsta quickly snatched his son up into his arms and realized he'd been shot in the head.

"*No. No. God, no. Fuck, no, no, no, no!*"

Gangsta started crying and rocking his son. The sirens were growing louder as he kissed Junior's face. He wanted to do something to help, but could think of nothing. He was heartbroken, holding his limp son in his arms. Gangsta was shattered. He was devastated to the point he didn't want to leave his family like this.

Erica was moving wildly, trying to get his attention. He looked at her, then back to his son. Gangsta put Junior down and went to help Erica. He could see the police lights starting to show from a short distance through the woods, so he went over and said, "Tell the police exactly what happened, and don't exclude nothing, ok?" Gangsta had tears running down his face. Erica nodded her head in reply, showing she understood. Gangsta quickly got up and got the duffel bag full of money and drugs, then slipped through the woods.

Chapter 2

Erica

Erica's entire body was numb from the morphine that pumped through the IV into her veins. It paralyzed her pains at the moment, and for that she was grateful, because it hurt badly both physically and mentally — physically from the beating she received and mentally from witnessing her sister and nephew being murdered in cold blood. Erica still could not believe out of all that happened, the men had the heart to kill a baby that was not even two years old, and to shoot him in the head was just low down and dirty. Thoughts of it mentally pained Erica to the point tears started to creep out of the corners of her eyes.

Don't exclude nothing, she remembered Gangsta saying before running into the woods.

Erica lay in the hospital bed healing from her wounds, thankful she was alive and had a second chance at life, but at the same time she was truly hurt, because Ne-Ne didn't get her second chance, nor the baby.

Erica was glad Gangsta killed them motherfuckers who did this. She watched in fear and admiration as Gangsta gunned down every last one of them and fled the scene. She knew he was hurt by the way he was crying when he talked to her. Erica saw it in his eyes that his heart was cold, his mind was out of place. *How could someone be so vicious?* she thought and looked around the hospital room.

The door was cracked, and she noticed two cops standing out front. There was a TV mounted on the wall inside the room, a glass vase sat on a table next to her bed, and the machines were on the other side.

The morphine had Erica drowsy. Her eyelids were getting heavy, and her heart was growing heavier from the losses. Erica found the remote next to the vase, and she turned the TV on and found the news channel. Her eyes closed once, her eyes closed twice, then she was out.

Ne-Ne was in the kitchen while Erica and Junior were in the living room watching SpongeBob. Erica was on the floor with Junior nested under her when a soft knock came at the door. She wondered who it could be, 'cause Ne-Ne hardly ever had company. She got up, leaving Junior looking at the TV, and walked to the door. Erica peeped out the side window to see a girl standing on the porch looking somewhat lost and nervous, which alarmed Erica. Her first thought was to ask Ne-Ne if she knew the girl who was knocking, but against her better judgment, she reluctantly opened the door, and it was the worst mistake Erica ever made.

Without warning, the door came crashing in, knocking Erica back. Two large dudes walked into the house, both holding guns, but neither had a mask. Erica tried to get up to no avail, because one of the big guys pounced on her.

"Bitch, where you going?" He punched Erica twice in the face with his massive fist, then harshly grabbed her hair. He was too big to put up a fight against, so she did the next best thing and screamed for Ne-Ne to get help. "Bitch, shut up!" The dude slapped her so hard it split her lip open.

Another guy walked into the house. He was a short, fat dude also holding a gun. Moments later, Erica saw Ne-Ne being held at gunpoint. When Ne-Ne saw that one of the guys had Junior in his arms, she panicked and went at her son. The fat guy surprised Erica with his speed and quickly detained Ne-Ne.

"Cuff these hos up," the biggest guy of them all said while still holding Junior. Erica and Ne-Ne were cuffed and duct tape was placed over their mouths. The girls were placed back-to-back on the living room floor. "Check the entire house. I will keep an eye on these two."

All the girls could do was mumble through the duct tape and kick out their feet. Nothing and nobody could help them at that moment, Erica thought, then she wondered what was going on and why. It didn't take the two guys long to come back up front with sweat pouring down their bodies.

"Everything clear," the fat dude said.

"Cool. Let's leave before a motherfucker try to be a hero. Get the kid." The biggest dude took Ne-Ne by her cuffed wrists, forcing her to her feet as the other guy grabbed Erica. Outside they were forced into an SUV, then black bags were put over their faces so they wouldn't know where they were going.

"Did you get the phones?" Erica couldn't see, but she heard one of the guys ask, then she remembered seeing the fat guy pocket her phone and Ne-Ne's phone.

"Yeah, I got both of 'em," somebody said.

"Ms. Robertson? Ms. Robertson?"

Erica opened her eyes to a blurry vision of people standing around her bed.

"Ms. Robertson."

She focused on the closest person to her, which was the doctor. Erica's eyes began to get heavy again.

"Yes?" Her throat was scratchy.

"Ms. Robertson, I'm Detective Gray, and this is Detective Brown. We know you have been through a rough day, but your help is needed. We need to know what exactly happened," the detective spoke, looking down at Erica.

"Excuse me, but my patient is heavily sedated right now and don't need nothing but some rest," the doctor cut in.

"That's understandable, but the longer we wait on her to heal, the less likely we will find those involved. I just have a few questions, then she can rest all she wants," Detective Brown stated, looking at the doctor like she was half crazy. The door swung opened and another doctor walked into the room. She spoke in a whisper to the first doctor. Meanwhile, the detectives were still trying to get information out of Erica.

"Listen, Ms. Robertson, you are the only person that can help us bring justice to what happened tonight. Your younger sister is in surgery, your nephew is on life support, so help us out. Give me some kind of clue to go on."

"My sister's in surgery?" Erica sat up in bed. "I thought Ne-Ne was—"

"Dead, we know. But no, she just took two bullets to the back," Detective Brown was happy to say.

Don't exclude nothing, she could still hear Gangsta say.

"What about Junior?"

"It's not his place to tell you nothing of that nature. Now what you need, young lady, is some rest so that you can heal up," the doctor spoke up, stepping in between the detectives and Erica.

"Well, I'm asking you, then. What's up with my nephew?" she turned to the doctor.

"We are uncertain as of now is all I can say, Ms. Robertson, so get some rest so that you—"

"Ok," Erica cut the doctor off. "But I gotta talk to the detectives first, so excuse us please," Erica said, which made the doctor open her mouth to protest, but she decided against it and left the room. Erica was so happy to hear the news of her sister being alive. She verbally made her statement to the detectives of what happened, from the door knock to the cemetery. She didn't leave out nothing, as Gangsta said. Erica did wonder why Gangsta would want her to tell on him, but at the same time she knew he had his reasons for doing the things he did.

After she made the statement, the detectives left, and a hour later Gangsta's face was all over the news for the triple homicide.

***

Veedo

Veedo couldn't believe Gangsta's face was all over the news, and for triple homicide is what most bothered him. Veedo wondered what happened, so fast and out of nowhere. Who was behind it? Or was Gangsta on a lick that went wrong?

As Veedo watched the news. the faces of two of Bam's bodyguards were among those killed, along with a baby being shot and now in critical condition. All this news confused Veedo. How did Bam get involved was the big question, because it was his bodyguards that were killed.

Leaving the TV when the news went to a commercial, he walked around the pod with many thoughts running through his head. Bam was low down, and Veedo sure hated the fact he trusted him so much. He should have known something wasn't right when Gangsta questioned him about Bam that day at the condo, but he wasn't thinking clearly at the moment. He was caught up in the fast money and unlimited drug supply. Now Veedo wished like hell he would've listened to Gangsta. Everybody he knew that sold drugs was booked by the Feds, and every day a new face entered the county jail. Veedo made his way over to an empty phone. This would be his first time reaching out to anybody, so he called the one he trusted most. His grandmother picked up and accepted his call.

"Baby boy?"

"What's going on, Ma? You ok?" Veedo asked genuinely

"God got me. But the question is are you ok?" His grandmother was quick on her feet, plus she knew her grandson like a book.

"Other than going back to prison, ma, I'm good. Do you remember the conversation we had, Ma?" he questioned.

"I surely do," she replied. His grandmother didn't forget anything. The last time Veedo saw her, he gave her money to put up and instructions on what to do in a time like this.

"Ok cool. So have you talked to April or seen the kids?" Veedo wanted to know, because he also left April, his babymama, some instructions if and when this happened, so he wanted to know what was up before court came up.

"April and the kids are safe. They will be over here later today, and yes, I made sure she packed all her bags as you requested. I also called our family lawyer, too. He's coming to see you soon," Veedo's grandmother said, but he didn't approve of that.

"Nah, ma. You know these Feds thinking I got all kind of money. I don't need no lawyer," Veedo replied, because he knew that all the Feds wanted was to catch him up with either drugs or money. As of that moment, they only had statements from Bam and Rock, which was enough to send him to the big house, but he didn't want to give them any more bullets to shoot him down.

"I know that, son. That's why he's our family lawyer, and can't no police do nothing about that. I'm not about to sit and watch you go to prison without putting up a fight. You have always been a fighter, so why stop the fight now?"

Veedo knew his grandmother was right. What would he lay down for? He came from a struggle, had fought some great battles in the form of obstacles, so continue to fight, right? He had enough money to handle whatever was needed. Veedo wasn't a fool. When he hustled, he grinded for a reason. Therefore, he stacked all his profits and never really spent unnecessary money. He was straight.

"You right, ma. Well, look, as soon as you can I want you to get down here, ok? I love you. I gotta go. Kiss my kids."

"I love you too, son," his grandmother replied.

Veedo got off the phone because intake had just dropped off some new guys in the pod, and one of them was Zay. Zay looked tired and fairly worried. His hair hadn't been cut, face unshaven, and clothes rumpled — he was looking rough. He was dragging his mat while holding a pillowcase filled with sheets, tissue, toothbrush, toothpaste, and a face towel. Veedo went to help, glad to see someone he knew and even more happy that now he could get the full swing on Bam.

"What da fuck going on, shawty?" Veedo asked, one-handed dapping Zay.

"The streets ugly," was all Zay could say as Veedo led him to a corner room. Inside the cell, Veedo put down the bag. Zay tossed the mat up on the bunk, then he leaned up against the wall. Veedo did the same opposite of him. Veedo saw stress written all over Zay's face like he had just gotten the worst news ever.

He finally looked up to Veedo and shook his head before saying, "Bruh, man, this nigga Bam is really on some mo' shit. Like real talk, bruh." He shook his head again with a scowl on his face. "This nigga, man. Damn!" Zay hit the wall behind him.

Veedo thought Zay was about to cry. He was so mad that tears were almost falling out of his eyes. Veedo knew the feeling of being crossed. He felt Zay's pain.

"What happened, bruh? What made the nigga flip?" Veedo asked.

"Shawty, all I know is we shopping in D.C. one morning, me, him, and his babymama Goldie. We left the mall and got pulled over 'bout two minutes later. Like them folks was watching us or something the whole time. Anyways, this nigga Bam had bricks in the trunk, bruh, like 600 rack just in the car, bruh. I'm talking stupid paper. Them Feds rolled up, bruh, I mean quick, and booked all of us, but the nigga Bam took the weight, shawty, and me and his ho hightailed it back to the city. A few days later, this nigga pop up, back to the basic," Zay said, shaking his head, clearly mad at himself.

"Did you question the nigga at all when he got back? Don't you think it was strange?" asked Veedo.

"Bruh, I just rolled wit' the flow 'cause the nigga freed me, so I didn't even bring the shit up. Even though I felt shit wasn't right, I still went with the flow. Fuck!" Zay hit the wall again.

"You heard about Gangsta and what's going on wit' him?" When Veedo asked that question, he saw something in Zay's eyes, something he couldn't read right then, but definitely something. Zay took a deep breath, shook his head, dropped his head, then looked up to Veedo.

"I fucked up, V. I didn't put Gangsta on point 'bout Bam when the nigga made plans to get at him. He felt like Gangsta disrespected him in the club, and another time they chopped it up. Really Bam didn't like how bluntly Gangsta turned him down, plus this shit wit' Pat Man didn't make it no better," Zay said.

"Damn, Zay," was all that came from Veedo's lips. He was stuck for words.

"Yeah, bruh, I know I fucked up. I fucked up big time. Dis nigga Bam is a dirty motherfucker, bruh, and I watched him put that hit in motion on Gangsta."

Veedo was still lost. He thought them niggas came up together, and it was messed up to side with an out-of-towner. He walked over to the cell door and looked out to the pod. He slid the door closed and posted back up on the wall before saying, "Didn't you and Gangsta come up together?" If Veedo could remember, that was the story Gangsta told him one day of him and Zay.

"Hell yeah, we—"

Zay couldn't finish his reply because Veedo caught him in the mouth with a quick two-piece that nearly knocked him out. The only thing that saved Zay from falling out was when he reached out and grabbed Veedo. Veedo got him again, but this time with a short, powerful blow to his nose. Veedo pushed Zay off him, took a step back, then grabbed his head, about to hit him with a viscous knee, but Zay grabbed his leg. By then the entire pod was tying to get a peek at the fight, which alerted the COs. Zay was trying to buck, but he couldn't because the very first blow had him dazed. Veedo caught Zay three times in the back with the bow until Zay let loose and dropped to the floor. As quickly as he could ease out the door, Veedo mixed in with the crowd of onlookers before the COs made it to the back where the fight took place.

Jerry Jackson

Chapter 3

Gangsta

"Anything you need is at your beck and call," Loco told Gangsta, standing behind him in the full-size mirror mounted on the living room wall. Gangsta had a big gash in his forehead that wouldn't stop bleeding and badly needed stitches. It was out of the question to go to a hospital, so he did the next best thing and applied pressure to the wound. Loco had picked Gangsta up on Perry Boulevard and taken him out to Gwinnett County to hide out at his sister's house because Gangsta's face was all over the news.

"Appreciate the love, Loco, real shit, way," Gangsta turned around and said, holding a towel to his head. It was hurting badly, but not as bad as the loss of his son and Ne-Ne. Gangsta wanted badly to go crazy, but knew he had to think things out because now all the attention was on him. Gangsta followed Loco into a den area where they both took seats. A maid walked in with food on a tray, smelling amazing. Gangsta had forgotten to even eat the past two days and really didn't care to eat now, though his body said different.

"Like I say, you will be safe here, way. Both my sisters stay here, which both are solid and already know you're here in hiding."

"I need a burn-out phone and a whip." Gangsta wasn't using his personal phone because he knew by now it was tapped, but he needed communication because Bam would not be getting away. Gangsta vowed to kill everybody Bam had love for.

"That's no problem," Loco replied with his best accent. As a knock came at the door, he excused himself, walking smoothly to the door. When he opened it, two more Mexicans walked in. They all dapped, then walked over to the table where Gangsta waited. Loco introduced the Mexicans as Jeter and Longo. They also took seats at the table.

"Gangsta need a untapped phone and a ride," Loco spoke to his two partners in Spanish.

"Consider it done," Jeter spoke back.

After they were served the food, Loco mostly talked to the Mexicans about moves being made while Gangsta's mind was on his family and how he let them down. His heart was heavy with sorrow, and it hurt to breathe at times. His daughter crossing his mind was the only thing that kept him sane, and the thought of revenge, as well. Gangsta's face was all over the news for triple homicide, but he wasn't worried. He stressed most about the whereabouts of Bam, because he couldn't afford to let Bam slip through without a fight.

Gangsta ate his food, then walked back to the living room where he had the duffel bag full of money and drugs. The only gun he had was the glock used to kill the kidnappers. He needed one bad — probably a couple guns going up against a stronger Bam who had a team, verses Gangsta being alone. Minutes later Loco, followed by his two friends, was heading out.

Loco stopped and said, "Either one of my sisters will be home soon. I must make a few runs, but will be back to check on you, my friend. And what you requested is on its way. Go do what you gotta do, and you're welcome back here. It's a safe place for you." Loco gave Gangsta dap.

"Say no mo', way." Gangsta most definitely was glad Kash linked him up with the Mexican. Loco proved to be much more than just business, and in Gangsta's book once loyalty was established, loyalty was owed. Gangsta looked down at the duffel bag, then said to Loco, "I got that money you fronted me, plus some. I wanna cop. Buy now and get later, though, until this nigga dead. Here is 700 racks. Take your two, and I'm spending five," Gangsta offered.

The gesture made Loco smile before saying, "Keep the money. Pay me back later, because in war you will need cash. Once you're done here and your legal matters get handled in your favor, then I bring you to meet my people. Good people, great business." Loco patted Gangsta's back. "Get well," then he headed out the door along with Jeter and Longo, leaving Gangsta alone in a place he wasn't use to being. Closing the duffel bag, Gangsta got up and decided to take a stroll through the massive crib. He pulled his shirt over his head with a struggle — a sharp pain was in his chest. Once the shirt was off, Gangsta pulled the vest straps apart and put the vest on a chair. Gangsta had two imprints on his chest from the bullets when they struck the vest. It almost hurt to breathe. Gangsta lightly touched the marks to test their tenderness. One thing was for sure: he couldn't get hit in his chest with anything else, not even a tennis ball.

Just when he was about to take his trip around the house, he noticed the same maid from dinner coming from the kitchen area. She smiled up at him and asked, "You need anything?" She was an older lady, but still held her beauty.

"I'm good," Gangsta replied. Then she walked off, but he stopped her. "I can use a shower, though."

The maid turned to him, smiled again, then said, "Follow me." She led him upstairs to a large room that he found to be a bathroom. "Towels are here." She pointed to a full-length mirror with handles on it. Gangsta slid it open to find stacks of face rags and body towels, soap, and shampoo also in the closet.

"Ok, thanks."

"No problem," the maid spoke, then exited the bathroom.

Maybe a shower was needed at that moment — something to wash the pain away that had a great big hold on him. Gangsta turned the water on and took a seat on the toilet, beginning to take off his shoes. A tear escaped his eye when he thought about his son and how he failed him. He was feeling less than a man since he could not take care of his son. He did not protect him as he should've, and it was getting to Gangsta in a major way. He stood up, taking off his pants. Another tear escaped his eyes, and this time Gangsta wiped it away. He took a deep breath and jumped in the shower.

After his shower, Gangsta had to put on the same clothes, just a different shirt. The shower felt great, something he had truly needed. It made him feel like a new man, but with the same agenda. While in the living room looking at the news, Gangsta heard the front door being tampered with, so he made a dash across the sofa for his glock, hoping it wasn't the police, because if it was, he was about to die or kill every last one of them. The knob to the door turned, then in walked a Mexican girl holding a Wal-Mart bag. Gangsta eased his hand off the gun and sat up straight on the plush leather sofa. The girl walked in and gave him a brief smile as she closed the door, then proceeded to the staircase, heading upstairs and not speaking a word. Gangsta noticed she was sexy as she disappeared, and moments later she came back down with the same bag.

"Sorry, I had to pee," she chuckled, then handed him the bag. "My hands are washed, too."

"Thanks." Gangsta took the bag and took a look inside. He found a flip phone and car keys. "What's your name?" he asked while pulling the phone out and powering it up.

"Melody," the Mexican girl said over her shoulder and again disappeared up the steps. The first person he called was his mother once he had the phone activated. Gangsta made sure not to call his mother's cell or home phone. He called a place he knew for certain the police didn't have tapped, which was her job. After he got someone on the phone, it took another minute for his mother to get on the line.

"Hello?"

"Ma." It was good to hear her voice. He was a bit relieved.

"Baby! Where are you? Are you ok?" He knew his mother had been worried about him, and even more now that he could hear it in her voice.

"Ma, they killed my son. They killed my girl. They tried to kill me, ma." Gangsta's voice cracked. He was breaking.

"I know, baby. Good news is they did not succeed in killing Ne-Ne or Junior, although he's on life support. He is still here, Gary. God is good. Just pray, baby, and be careful—"

"Junior's alive?" He cut her off with questions of excitement. It was in his tone. "Ne-Ne's alive?"

"Ne-Ne successfully made it out of surgery, Erica is down in recovery, and Junior is on life support. The doctors want us to pull the plug, but have to have the parents' consent. They say it's no possible way Junior will make it without life support," his mom said.

The news made him thankful, but at the same time even more mad. Gangsta didn't believe for one second what the doctors were saying about his son.

"When Ne-Ne wakes up, tell her don't pull no plug on my son. I gotta go, ma. Meet me at the place you said you and my dad met. I will be there when you get off. Love you, Ma," Gangsta said and quickly hung up, still paranoid. Even though his mother worked at the hospital, the phones being tapped crossed his mind all of a sudden. The news that Ne-Ne and Junior were still alive gave Gangsta more life. He had more bounce to his step as he pocketed the phone.

Melody came back down the steps holding a suitcase. Gangsta was strapping his vest on when their eyes met. Something about her beauty captivated him at moments, though his focus most definitely wasn't on the fact she was a female, but he still could not deny she was bad.

"Loco called and asked did you need any assistance? He could send Jeter and Longo to help you out," Melody spoke once she sat the suitcase down. Her English was clear, but her native tone was still there.

"Tell him I'm good right now, but thanks," Gangsta replied, appreciating the love, but he would much rather do everything solo thanks to Dank's bitch-ass.

"He figured you would say that, so he wanted you to have this." She picked up the suitcase and handed it toward him. "This should help."

Gangsta took it and opened it to find two assault rifles, three handguns, and extra clips with bullets. He closed it back, then looked up to the beautiful Mexican girl. "Tell bruh good looking."

"I will," Melody said and left him to his space. Gangsta looked at the time and took out some money and all the bricks. He had to get in the streets if he wanted to catch Bam or anybody with him before it was to late.

***

Ne-Ne

As soon as her eyes opened, the police were hovering over her bed. She quickly closed her eyes to envision the last thing she remembered. Ne-Ne's eyes reopened.

"Junior! Where is my son?" She looked around both detectives as if her son was somewhere in the room, but saw nobody. "Where is my son?" Panic started to set in as she questioned them. One of the detectives walked closer to the bed and cleared his throat.

"Mrs. Robertson, do you recall anything that happened to you?" Detective Gray was the one that spoke.

Ne-Ne looked at him. She could remember everything up until she was shot. She tried to sit up, but to no avail as pain shot through her stomach, causing her to look down at herself to see her stomach had tubes running through it. Ne-Ne quickly closed her eyes again before asking, "Where is my sister? My son?"

The room door opened and in walked the doctor, which suddenly stopped the questions aimed at the detectives. Ne-Ne focused her eyes on the older doctor. "My son, where is he?"

"Mrs. Robertson, your son is in our intensive care unit. He's living off life support, and your consent is needed—"

"Life support!" Despite the tubes in her stomach, Ne-Ne sat up, not believing her ears and not feeling the pain, either.

"Your son was shot in the head. Did you not know that?" the doctor asked.

"Shot in the head!" Ne-Ne tried desperately to get up as tears came pouring out of her eyes. Her whole world was shattered as the reality of things started to set in. The doctors moved in to help Ne-Ne sit back correctly.

"Easy. You have fresh wound and fifty-four staples we don't want to bust open," the doctor said while Ne-Ne pushed her hands out of the way, still trying to move and crying historically.

"No, no, no! Oh my God, this can't be happening. God, no!" Ne-Ne pushed and pulled. The doctor asked the detectives to leave so they could calm Ne-Ne down. More nurses rushed into the room. As the detectives left, they put some sleeping medicine in Ne-Ne's IV, and seconds later she was out cold.

Ne-Ne didn't know if she was dreaming or not when she awoke and saw Erica standing by her bedside. Erica smiled when she notice her sister's eyes finally flutter open. Ne-Ne saw Keshana and Terry also, along with Mrs. Jackson. Balloons, flowers, and bears filled the table by the window. Ne-Ne's mouth was dry, her throat was scratchy, but it did not stop her from questioning, "Where is my son?"

Ne-Ne looked to anyone for answers, and her heart got heavy when she saw the sorrowful look on everyone's face. She instantly started shaking her head, running back into her denial state. "No, no. Don't tell me." Ne-Ne began to cry. Gangsta's mother stepped in as Erica also got up and took ahold of her sister's hand.

"Nya, baby, Junior was shot in the head. He is brain dead, as it reads, so I need you to be strong for him, let God handle everything, 'cause he can. I need you with a level head, baby," Mrs. Jackson said, running her hand over Ne-Ne's teary face, moving the hair that threatened to embrace the tears that rolled easily down her cheeks.

"Sis, you know I'm here, girl. I promise we will get through this," Erica added the best words of encouragement she could muster. She was also devastated by the loss, but not as much as Ne-Ne must been. Everybody and their mom knew that Ne-Ne adored her son. Erica wasn't a mother, so this pain she wouldn't feel as her sister was feeling, though she vowed to cry with her, laugh with her, and was even willing to go crazy with her if need be. It was the least she could do. for the next ten minutes, they all just sat there in silence as Ne-Ne cried her eyes out. Mrs. Jackson dropped a tear also, because she wasn't a stranger to the feeling of losing a child. Everything came to a stop when the head doctor walked in. She had a folder in her hand. She was a older white lady with a head full of white hair. She wore a warm smile on her face as she approached Ne-Ne's bedside, opening the folder.

"Your surgery was a success. We was able to remove both bullets with ease—"

"What's going on with my motherfucking son?" Ne-Ne's voice became high pitched, her face turning red. she wasn't trying to hear all the beating-around-the-bush tails. She wanted answers.

"Your son is brain dead, bullet shot to the head. There's nothing we can do at this point. Because he's just a baby, he will not put up the fight a grown-up would," the doctor said, pulling a sheet of paper from the folder. "We need your consent to take him off life support." She tried to give Ne-Ne the paper and quickly got it knocked out of her hand to the floor.

"Leave my son on the machine," stated Ne-Ne with a mean scowl on her pretty face, nose at a flare, face going beat red. She was ready to hurt someone at that moment, preferably her baby daddy for even putting them in a situation so crazy.

The other doctor bent down to retrieve the paper, at the same time saying, "Ma'am, your insurance doesn't even cover us to keep running the machine. It will cost you so much money to keep going when the results will be the same a month from now. Your son is suffering right now—"

"Leave the fancy machine running. His father will get it paid. Now get the fuck out of my room!" Ne-Ne demanded with a point of her finger.

Jerry Jackson

Chapter 4

Gangsta

When Gangsta made it to Atlanta, he rode up and down Bankhead and Hollywood Road in search of anybody who would know anything or was connected to Bam in any way possible. He was looking high and low, but doing so in a smooth manner not to be noticed by anyone who wasn't helpful. On the ride from Gwinnett to Atlanta, he heard over the radio that there was reward money out for any info on his whereabouts. Gangsta refused to be caught like that, because he wouldn't be successful in getting to Bam. After an hour of driving the Westside streets, mind in limbo, Gangsta decided to pull up on Nikki, Terry's best friend. She had an apartment in Dogwood, off Banked Highway. Gangsta knocked on the door, making sure to keep his head down, fitted cap pulled over his eyes. He wore all black clothing that mixed in with the night skies as time began to lap over. Gangsta heard the door rattle as it cracked opened, and his eyes met Poonie's, Nikki's deadbeat baby daddy who was in and out of jail. Poonie stepped to the side to let Gangsta in.

"What's up, shawty?" Poonie asked, surprised to see the man of the hour. Gangsta entered the crib, taking in the few people in the living room: Roxanne and another girl he didn't recognize. Nikki was also there, and she stood to her feet as soon as she saw it was Gangsta at her door.

"What's hap', Poonie? What's up, Nikki, Roxanne?" Gangsta spoke.

Nikki, on the other hand, walked over and hugged him, then looked at the big gash in his forehead before saying, "Glad to see you alive, Gangsta. You need stitches, you know?"

"That's not important right now, but I'm good, thanks. Look, I can't hang long, but I'm looking for Bam, and I need y'all's help," Gangsta said.

"So Bam behind all this?" asked Roxanne.

"Something like dat."

"Shawty got a babyma who stay on Lucile Avenue that's all I know."

Poonie added, "Step and Monkey work for him. Them two niggas who the Feds ain't snatched up, and they still eating around here when nobody moving." He held a blunt in his hand, and he passed it to Gangsta. Gangsta in return looked at Poonie then took the blunt.

"Where can I find them?" was Gangsta's question.

"Oh, them niggas got a spot on Cleveland Avenue," replied Poonie.

"And his babymama, do you got the address to both spots?" Gangsta hit the blunt once and passed it back.

"Yeah, not the address, but I can explain or better yet point them shits out for you, my nigga. That was some fuck shit Bam pulled to shoot your son, plus me and you, we came up in these streets together," Poonie said without hesitation, and Gangsta took notice. It earned Poonie some points in his book, because he didn't have to say shit. True enough, him and Gangsta came up in the same hood, but he really didn't fuck with Poonie like that. It was just how the hood was: everywhere it's niggas and bitches that didn't get spoken to or messed with, but now Poonie was willing to help him.

He and Gangsta jumped in the rental Loco gave Gangsta and flooded the streets. The ride over was mostly Poonie talking and Gangsta listening while his mind focused on his son. He also wondered how Ne-Ne and Erica were holding up. *I'ma get revenge for y'all,* Gangsta thought to himself as Poonie directed him through the Atlanta streets. The first stop was made on Lucile Avenue, where Bam had a young, stripper babymama named Goldie. When they got there, the house was vacated. Gangsta questioned two different people he met while lingering, and both said that Goldie just up and left, but only one said they had contact on her. Gangsta wasted no time buying the info and got her cell number. The very next stop was Cleveland Avenue to holla at Step and Monkey. It was a crowd of niggas posted outside when Gangsta and Poonie parked and approached the fence, entering the yard.

"Looking for Step and Monkey," Gangsta said, not being formal, but straight to the point. One of the many guys in the yard walked up. He eyed both Poonie and Gangsta before speaking.

"Who y'all niggas is, pulling up asking police questions? Ain't no Monkey or Step over in dis trap." Dude was feeling himself, Gangsta noticed.

"Check this out, bruh, ain't no beef, no disrespect, no nothing, bruh. I'm just trying to meet these two niggas and I'm out."

"Well, you in the wrong place. Like I said, ain't no Monkey—"

"Gary! Gary Gangsta motherfucking Jackson!"

Gangsta turned at the sound of his government name being called. He saw the dude walking toward, him but couldn't place his face. The smile the dude held assured him that everything was cool, or he hope so.

"It's Jay, my nigga!" He held his hand out toward Gangsta, who shook it.

"Damn, bruh, what's up?" Gangsta was surprised to see him, but also happy to know someone over here.

"Been out 'bout two weeks now. Come on in, my nigga, it's all love." Jay began to introduce Gangsta to everyone, telling them him and Gangsta met in the pen. Gangsta quickly found out that Monkey and Step were two of the many niggas who were there, so after the introductions Gangsta wasted no time.

"Let me holla at y'all two." Gangsta pointed both of them out. Without hesitation, Monkey and Step led him to one of the back rooms. Inside, after they closed the door, Gangsta turned around to face them.

"I'ma be honest with y'all, my nigga. Right now I got a death wish. I'm on some kill-me shit at this moment. Bam, he's y'all connect, I know and I respect that, but Bam's ass finna die. See, my son ain't but two, and my nigga sitting on life support 'cause he took a bullet to the head. I'm being real when I say I never had beef wit' that nigga. He just hot 'cause I didn't get on his team, next thing you know my family is kidnapped. Look, like I said, he's your connect. Well, I will do y'all better prices, better dope. cause I'm the plug in Atlanta, 'cause this nigga gotta go. I need some info on this sucka. I got four kilos right now, and I will connect y'all niggas so your money won't stop when this bitch on ice."

Both Monkey and Step looked at each other, then back to Gangsta.

"Four bricks?" Step asked.

"Right now, bruh. I just wanna murk this bitch for what he did to my son." Gangsta was desperate, and they saw it in his eyes.

"My nigga, I'm not gone even lie, I feel where you coming from, but we gotta think about this shit. I mean, you just want us to give up a sweet connect for a sweeter mojo, but it's not that simple, bruh." Monkey spoke.

Then Step added, "Yeah, 'cause we don't know you from a can of paint, and you asking us the unthinkable."

"Shawty, just put yo'self in my shoes. This nigga Bam is a rat, bruh. He a crossout artist, my nigga, and the streets know. I'm telling y'all niggas first hand that I will give y'all better prices and dope. The nigga gon' die anyway, whether now or later," Gangsta pressed.

"Just let us give this shit some thought," Step said.

Even though Gangsta felt defeated, he still managed a smile. He wanted to do the both of them badly, but spared them for two reasons: they was way too deep in the house and Poonie wasn't on point. This is where he missed Kash, 'cause if Gangsta popped it off in the back, Kash would pop it off in the front. Gangsta left the trap spot with plans to return, but when and if he did it would not be nice. He dropped Poonie off and headed to meet his mother.

Gangsta pulled up an hour late, but she was still there waiting for her son with his daughter. When Keshana saw her father, she screamed and jumped from her grandmother's lap, running to her Daddy. Gangsta scooped her up and kissed her jaw and nibbled her neck. Keshana giggled under her dad's attention. His mother also got up to embrace her baby boy. She wrapped her arms around his shoulders. It was a hug he needed, the love he was missing, and Gangsta broke down in tears. He was hurt beyond words, and she knew it. The only other time she'd witnessed her son cry like this was when Cool died.

"It's ok to cry, baby." She rubbed his back as his daughter wiped the tears that fell. Every time Gangsta dropped his head, Keshana would push it back so she could see her dad crying. It made Gangsta laugh at her effort, but the tears still kept flowing.

"I feel helpless, ma. I don't know what to do. I wanna help my son, but I can't. Ne-Ne's mad, probably hates my guts. I didn't protect them, ma," Gangsta said through the tears

"Well, baby, Ne-Ne isn't mad at you. She loves you. She is just stubborn and hurt, just as much as you are. Junior will not make it, though. Baby, the both of y'all gotta let the baby rest. I know it's hard, but it's a decision y'all are forced to make," Mrs. Jackson spoke, but Gangsta shook his head, still in denial. He put his daughter down. Life had never been this harsh for him.

"Call my lawyer, ma. Tell him money is sent, but go ahead and start working. Go get statements from Erica and Ne-Ne. I'm not turning myself in until I get this nigga though, ma, or I'ma die trying," He spoke through his anger.

"Don't say that, baby, and I've already talked to Swinn. He's on his job. You just be safe, Gary, and do not get caught doing nothing else. And you need stitches, baby." His mother reached for his face, but Gangsta moved out of reach like he was a lil' kid again.

"I'm good, ma." Gangsta gave his mother some money and a tape recorder. That made her raise an eyebrow until he assured her it was for the detectives when they questioned her or Ne-Ne.

"Gary, I'm not about to let my son walk around with a big-ass gash in his face. I have the things in my car to stitch you up. It will only take a minute."

Gangsta wanted to put up a fight, but knew he would lose, and that would be more time wasted. He let her do her motherly duties while his daughter helped, then Gangsta headed back to Gwinnett County to think up a master plan.

Chapter 5

Gangsta

"I need to take a trip to Miami," Gangsta announced once he walked into the house in Gwinnett. Loco was seated on the sofa, piles of money covered the table, and stacks were on the floor. Melody and another Mexican girl were wrapping red plastic around the money. Jeter and Longo were over in the den stuffing pounds of weed into boxes, moving at a rapid pace. Nobody but Loco looked up at Gangsta's statement.

"I take it you need me to get you there?" Loco questioned.

"Most definitely would be grateful," honestly Gangsta admitted. He was pressed for time. He needed the help now.

"I have people who can check things for you first, that's if you want, so that your trip won't be in vain. Plus I got intel that Bam is still in the city. Word is he can't leave until this trial is over, but until then he's under FBI supervision. I'm not saying he will not strike or that he's not pushing the work, 'cause all that's possible, it's just he's not on the scene. And where he's at is the big question for both of us, my friend," Loco said. He reached in his pocket and pulled out a rolled blunt. He put some fire to it, hit it a couple times, then passed it to Gangsta.

"So, can you find out if this nigga's baby's mother in hiding down there?" Gangsta asked. He wanted to be sure he was hearing right. He hit the blunt also and instantly felt the high he needed. He needed his nerves calmed. Loco stood.

"Just a phone call away, that's it," he said. Gangsta passed the blunt back. He hoped Loco could pull that move off. He also hoped there was truth in Bam being in Atlanta still, because it made it all the much better, but first things first, he needed to know the truth.

Loco and Gangsta walked into the den. Loco started helping Jeter and Longo load pounds of loud weed in boxes. Gangsta followed lead after only a second. It took them over an hour to pack sixteen boxes and for the girls to wrap two mil and also pack them into boxes. Gangsta helped load everything into a van inside of the garage. Within the time spent around everyone, Gangsta got introduced to Loco's younger sister, Mya. She was far prettier than Melody, she just wasn't as thick, but she proved to be just as cool.

"Ok, it's confirmed that Bam's baby mother is indeed in Miami at her parents' spot. Jeter and Longo will take this trip with you, give you the support you need. I will have a change of cars for you there in Miami and a place to lay low at until this issue is resolved, but do not get comfortable and think he won't pull one of his stunts, so get in and out of Dade County," Loco spoke from the driver seat of the van.

"'Preciate it," Gangsta said, and he really meant that. Loco left with both of his sisters, leaving the three of them to devise a plan on what they needed to do before they even took the trip. Longo was the thinker. He was the one almost always saving the situations as they occurred. Jeter was the hothead and hardly ever socialized, all he wanted was money. Jeter was the youngest, and Gangsta could tell by the many tattoos that covered his body and face. Gangsta learned that Longo was on the run from Mexico for a string of murders he committed just to prove himself to Loco's father, Chavez, a major drug kingpin. After talking a minute about Miami, Gangsta excused himself to use his cellphone. He dialed his mother's number. She picked up just as quickly as he called.

"Ma," he didn't give her a chance to say hello, "Ma, where you at?" Gangsta asked. Both Longo and Jeter were preparing to leave, waiting on him. Gangsta grabbed his gun from the table.

"On my way back to the hospital," she replied.

"Ok, listen, ma, do not by any means go back home. I'm sending someone to escort you to auntie's house, 'cause this nigga is still in the city and he may try to come at you." Panic could be heard in his voice, and his mother peeped it. Gangsta loved his mom, and if something was to happen to her on his account, he wouldn't know what to do. It was already almost impossible for him, dealing with his son being on life support. He couldn't take another blow.

"Ok, son, that's fine by me. I'm at South Fulton Hospital. Erica is being released today, too. Should I take her along?"

"Yeah, ma. Keshana and Terry, too," Gangsta said.

"Ok, 'cause Terry is at the hospital with Ne-Ne, so we will be waiting for our escort." After hanging up the phone, he went to retrieve his duffel bag, where he took out a brick of cocaine. Longo and Jeter looked at each other, then to Gangsta as if he was crazy.

"What's that for?" Longo asked, curious.

"I need to drop this to a few shooters I know to move my folks to a safe place," Gangsta replied, then added, "Ain't no telling how long we gon' be in Miami. I'ma need Niggas to watch my peoples."

"Listen," Jeter spoke, "we can get people on your family, you'll just owe us. Put that kilo back. We got to hit the road. Don't worry about your mom, she will be safe," he said and made the call right in Gangsta's face, which gave him comfort, and right then and there he vowed to stay fuckin' with them, because he saw first-hand they were about their issues and money. Gangsta didn't say another word, he just went with the flow.

***

Bam

Sweat poured from the dude's body as he shook uncontrollably, scared for the life he knew he would soon lose. He was duct taped and chained to a chair, badly beaten, both eyes swollen shut from the many blows he'd recently received.

"Snatch that fuck-nigga's head back, yo," Bam ordered Monkey, who was looking almost as scared as the dude in the chair, but did not hesitate standing behind the dude. Monkey had a rope held tight in both hands. He tossed it around the neck of the boy and pulled back hard, exposing nothing but a clear shot for a sure kill. Bam smiled to himself, then looked over to Step, who held a stony look on his face, eyes never leaving the guy in the chair. Bam walked over to his cream leather sofa. He reached under it, coming out with an all-chrome axe. Bam admired the art in his hand for a moment, then spoke.

"Yo, I always wanted to use one of these motherfuckers. This some nice shit, son," Bam said to nobody in particular while walking back over to the guy in the chair. He sat the axe against the side of the man's leg. Bam looked around his massive living room. His three bodyguards stood off to the side, each holding semi-automatic weapons. Bam's young ho, Trina, was also posted, and Monkey and Step were the only people other than the dude in the chair inside the house. The Feds were parked outside his house in two unmarked cars.

"See, it's niggas like you I dislike: un-loyal motherfuckers, pussy-niggas, and traders that fuck the game up and knock shit down before it can go up. Nigga, I put you on your feet. I turned you up and blessed you with love, and you embrace the enemy? You go against codes that only ho-niggas break, and hos not allowed in my circle." Bam walked back and forth, and in between strides he would stop to look at the dude, helpless in the chair.

Bam was hardcore in everything he did, but was most vicious with his murder game. He grew up with a killer's blood running through his veins, and being raised in the heart of Brooklyn didn't help him. Bam was only fourteen when he killed his first person. He was with Lucky and had to prove himself before the kingpin of Brooklyn. Murder was his thing, but money had always been his motivation, so with the two he quickly became powerful — a power he once shared with Lucky, but New York wasn't big enough for them both once Bam's pants got too big for him. Even though the love was real and the respect was there, they both held different views and could never seem to agree or connect. Since leaving New York, Bam had taken over four different states' major cities, putting his stamp down and plugging with some serious connections outside of being given the cheapest prices on all of Lucky's drugs. Bam couldn't even count the bodies he had under his belt, he just knew it was many.

"Never cross the one that feed you, for the one you felt sorrow for, and that goes for everybody," Bam said while picking the axe up. He held it in both hands, raised it up, placing the sharp blade aimed at the dude's exposed throat. Bam gritted his teeth and drew the axe back.

Monkey wanted to close his eyes.

Step just looked, saying nothing at all.

Bam swung the axe with force from his 175-pound frame. The blade sliced through the dude's neck, ripping his head off. Blood gushed out in spurts.

Bam smiled and said, "I always wanted to use this bad boy." He dropped the axe at his feet. "And to let y'all niggas know, son, I know that bitch-nigga Gangsta offered a pack to turn me over. Not a wise choice if you even considered it. This nigga is a peon compared to me, and I want him dead, caught and killed, plus anybody who got love for this sucka. And when it's done, I will double the ticket."

Both Monkey and Step nodded their heads in agreement, but were still shocked at what Bam just did. Bam had them put the body in a deep freezer.

"Damn, Jay," Monkey said when he closed the deep freezer with his friend inside. It hurt him the most because Jay was his baby mother's brother. Monkey knew he couldn't even look in her eyes after this day.

Bam looked out the window of his ten-bedroom house in Mount Zion, GA, tucked off in a very low-key neighborhood. Two FBI cars sat in his driveway, still taking pictures. He would find a way to duck them today when they tried to follow him. Right now he didn't need the Feds breathing down his neck.

Bam closed the curtain back and walked over to his cherry wood dresser to remove his jewels. He noticed spots of blood on his face and on his clothes. *Blood of a sucka,* Bam thought to himself. Stripping down to his boxers, he took a seat on his California king bed, picking up his phone, checking to see if his baby mother made it to Miami safe. There wasn't a call or a text. Bam hated when people didn't do as he instructed them to do. He tossed the phone back on the bed as the double doors to his bedroom opened up and in walked Trina, his young rider. Trina was twenty-four with a body to kill for and ass for days, but it wasn't the looks that attracted Bam to the five foot, four inch, pecan tan beauty. It was her gangsta. Trina wouldn't hesitate under pressure.

"Daddy, the body been dumped and them niggas cleaning up. One of them FBI guys asked to use the restroom, but we didn't let him in. I got the driver ready to pull off on your call," Trina said while taking a seat on the bed, admiring what she saw. Bam was tatted up all over his back, his chest, and arms. It was so sexy to her, and always she let it be known by the way she stared at him. Lust was what always captivated her. Even though the love was pure, her lust was a big part of her loyalty, and Bam knew this.

"Yo, shorty, you looking at a nigga like a piece of meat, ma," Bam laughed

"You are my meat, nigga," she bluntly replied and got up, walking toward him, stopping face-to-face. "And I'm whatever you need me to be," Trina said honestly, because Bam was truly all she had as far as family. They met one night at the strip club Magic City, where she danced. She was nineteen then, with the stripper name Stacks. Bam did not wait another minute, snatching her off the market, off stage, out of the club. He promised to take care of all her needs and wants. Bam said he knew she was a solider, not a dancer

"Yo, ma, you by far the prettiest solider I've seen, and I'm here to save you from the wicked world, to place heaven at your feet." She remembered his words vividly, even though it'd been years. She still held dear to his word, and he'd kept it so far. Bam kissed her face. "I'm 'bout to hop in this shower, ma. Go grab me something fly to put on, and you get sexy, too. If the Feds gonna watch us, then let them bitches see us fly." Trina smiled. "Ok, Daddy, I'm on it." She kissed his chest and disappeared into his thirty-by-twelve walk-in closet equipped with the latest fashions.

Bam's mind was consumed with his next move in life as he bathed under the hot water. After this take-over in Atlanta and once Gangsta was out of the picture, Bam had plans to relocate his empire and start new where nobody knew him. He knew the Feds would be forever crawling up his back, so Bam kept something for them at all times. When shit got real, he would be ready. See, he didn't care about someone calling him a rat, a snitch, or whatever because he was a millionaire, and that was facts. None of his real, true friends liked that. Bam was so quick to cross niggas out on police shit, but Bam always said, "Yo, son, them niggas will tell on me any time the pressure is applied. These slow-ass niggas don't like New York niggas, so fuck them first before they fuck me. That's word, son."

Lucky never spoke on it. He wasn't worried at all if Bam tried to snitch him out. He had the correct people in the perfect places to make any and everything disappear. Lucky still dealt with Bam because of a promise he made to Bam's father before he died to see his son through. Bam's father was Lucky's mentor and the guy who gave Lucky the vision he had, and Lucky was the type of person to stick to his word.

Bam stepped out of the shower, shaking thoughts of Lucky out of his mind. A soft knock came at the door. It was Trina, and she walked in holding his cellphone. Bam took it.

"Yo."

"We made it, Bernard," his baby's mother spoke the words Bam had been waiting to hear. He was happy she was out of Georgia, but he instantly got mad because she'd been ignoring his calls.

"Yo, why you not been picking up the phone, shorty?" he questioned while standing naked in front of Trina.

"No service, Bernard. You actually think I would ignore your calls?" was his babymama's reply. Bam just smiled it off, because he was glad to hear her voice. He moved past Trina into his bedroom.

"Ok, cool. I'm glad you safe. Yo, where is my shorties?" he wanted to know.

"Sleep. That trip was long, baby. I will have them call you when they get up. Is that fine, or do I need to wake them?"

"No, you good, ma. Love you. I will call back later," Bam said and ended the call. After another minute, he and Trina got dressed in some fly gear and headed downstairs where Monkey and Step awaited him with his bodyguards.

Chapter 6

Erica
The Next Day

Erica was packing the last of her things when her room door opened and in walked the two detectives. She rolled her eyes at just the mere sight of them, already overwhelmed with their pressure. Erica took a seat on the bed.

"Now what?" was her question.

"Good morning, Mrs. Robertson," Detective Brown was the first to speak, at the same time pulling a statement form from his folder. "We need to know exactly what happened the night you were kidnapped." At first she just looked at the detectives, looked so hard it seemed she was looking through them, like they were becoming a blur to her eyes. Erica was tired, worried, and confused. She shook her head.

"I don't remember anything," she spoke in a mumble — a mumble that made both detectives look at each other as if she had lost her mind.

Detective Brown cleared his throat. "We have a verbal statement from you confessing that Gary Jackson was the one who killed your kidnappers.

"I was drugged up. I don't remember," Erica said and stood to her feet. Ne-Ne didn't want her talking to the cops. She made that very clear last night when Erica eased into her room. Both sisters cried about Junior, had a long, detailed talk about what was the best move to be made concerning her son. Erica witnessed so much pain in her younger sister as she decided not to help the police.

"The guys who kidnapped us are dead already, so why is you telling on Gangsta? All the police gonna do is lock him up. That do not help us, it hurt us, 'cause now he can't save his son nor get the bitch who sent the hit. I got just one day to decide on Junior's

conditions, and it's to keep the machine running. I'd rather die than see my son's funeral," Ne-Ne said, and Erica knew she was right.

"Mrs. Robertson, are you saying that statement you made was false?" Detective Grey asked.

"That's exactly what I'm saying, but I will make one now."

"Giving us a detailed story of what happened?"

"The only statement I can make is that I do not remember," Erica stressed as she moved around the detectives, gathering her things to leave. She could tell by the looks on their faces she had them both pissed off.

"Ok, fine, Mrs. Robertson. If you want to begin to play dumb, then that's on you. All we're trying to do is help you and your family, but it won't get done with you and your sister acting stubborn, so when and if you remember anything, then give us a call," Grey spoke, passing Erica his card. Erica didn't say anything, just watched them leave, and was happy they did. She began to finish packing her things. She had plans to stay with her sister until she also recovered. Being kidnapped was a wake-up call for her. All she could think about were the things she hadn't done with her sister yet. Everything crossed her mind, giving her the wake-up she needed. It wasn't long after the detectives left that two Mexicans entered her room, which instantly made her heart drop. She wasn't strong enough to put up a fight, and she had nowhere to go. All she could think about was screaming for help. One of the Mexicans saw the situation was about to get out of hand, so he put his hands out.

"Ma'am, Gangsta sent us," he spoke in a low tone to let her know she didn't have to panic. The door opened again, and this time Terry walked in with a worried look on her face. Mrs. Jackson was also walking into the room.

"What's going on?" Erica asked, now confused more than ever.

"We may be in danger, so Gary sent an escort for us. We all are going to my sister's house until this situation is resolved," Mrs. Jackson gave Erica understanding.

"Where is my sister?" Erica wanted to know.

"She's in recovery. Them detectives are in there trying to get statements," Terry said.

"I'm not leaving my sister's side, Mrs. Jackson. Tell Gangsta thank you, but I'm only leaving this hospital when Ne-Ne does."

"Ma'am, your sister will be looked after 24/7. Nothing will happen to her," one of the Mexicans spoke. He was a short, older Mexican with gray hair all over his head. The other one had yet to speak. He was taller with ripped muscles, and at all times he stood with his hands behind his back.

"Trust me, there's enough of them here, Erica, to watch Nya and the baby. Gangsta just wants us all to be safe." Terry put one of her hands on Erica's shoulder.

"Your sister will be safe, ma'am. I promise," the Mexican said, again leaving Erica no choice but to go with the plan at hand. She just wanted her family safe.

"Ok, but I need to see my sister before I go." Erica looked at Gangsta's mom, then to the Mexicans. Both of them shook their heads in agreement. When Erica walked into the hallway, there were a few more Mexicans outside the door. She instantly felt better about her sister's safety and secure about leaving Ne-Ne with them. The elevator ride up was quiet. She was led to her sister's room, and there were three more Mexican men standing outside her room. She didn't knock, she walked straight in on the detectives tossing question after question at Ne-Ne.

***

Veedo

Today was his first court appearance since being arrested a few weeks ago. Today would either make or break him. Today he would find out exactly what was going on with this case.

Veedo, along with three more inmates, was escorted down to the transfer floor and pushed into holding cells with many more niggas heading to court to get their bad or good news. Would they go home? Would they stay? When Veedo was pushed into one of the holding tanks, he saw many nervous faces, and even a few familiar faces. One of the guys he noticed was Eric, Gangsta's cousin, and boy was he looking nervous. Veedo walked over.

"What's up, homie?" He stuck his hand out for some dap and got it.

"Coolin', bruh," replied Eric.

"You heard anything good 'bout Gangsta? You heard what happened, right?"

"Hell yeah, I heard. All I keep seeing on the news is that he's wanted for murder, and the media trying to make Ne-Ne out to be an unfit mother," Eric added, because the media had Ne-Ne on the news channel looking like a bad person when in reality she was a sweet soul. Veedo just shook his head. He also took a seat on the steel bench that was packed with niggas, plus more inmates were being pushed into the already tight room.

"So what's up? Do you got any defense against these crackers?" Veedo wanted to know. Did Eric have any loopholes in his case? Even though he had been to prison already, it wasn't the Feds.

"I know I'm not taking no plea. Not right now, no way. My cousin is out there lurking, and best believe shawty finna find and kill Bam. Bam the only thing the Feds got on us. Shit, if cuz can pull this off quick enough, then this shit gets beat," Eric told him.

It didn't take long for Veedo to decide to follow Eric's lead, because he was right. If Gangsta offed Bam, then all Veedo would have to worry about was Rock and Kia's statements. It wasn't long before they arrived at the courthouse and Veedo met up with his lawyer. They shared a quick talk, which made Veedo feel better about facing the judge. They really didn't have any solid evidence on any of the guys, just hearsay, and with a good enough lawyer they could get off.

Veedo's name was called an hour later. He entered the courtroom with his head held high and heart in the pit of his stomach. He was happy to see his grandmother and April, his babymama, there to support him. He winked at them both as he and his lawyer addressed the court. The Feds had him charged with conspiracy and money laundering through three counties. The judge asked him how he pled, and his lawyer said not guilty. The judge set him another date after he denied bond and dismissal, but Veedo was good with that. He wasn't worried about nobody but Gangsta.

He was led back into the holding cell. Veedo made up his mind that he was just gonna sit back and ride this wave, and if he had to go to the Feds, he would try to get a small amount of time. In the next holding cell over, he saw Zay and Rock with a few more niggas waiting for their names to be called. Zay's face was swollen badly, which made Veedo smile at the beat down he gave him. Veedo locked eyes with Rock and shook his head at what he saw. If looks could kill, Rock would drop dead where he stood. Pure hate was painted on Veedo's face, and Rock had to walk off feeling like the fuck-nigga he was. Veedo laughed and walked away, too. He knew before it was over with, he would see Rock again, but this time it would be gun-blazing, bodies-dropping, because there were rules in the game, and snitching was a number one no-no.

***

Monkey

"Nigga, you sure this the spot?" Monkey asked Step while looking at the large, gated house sitting far back from the streets. They were far out in Smyrna, Georgia. It was a place thugs weren't seen, and when or if they were seen, it was a red flag. Both guys were strapped, both on papers, so they had to be extra careful. The police lay in wait in this area. Any day a thug could get booked.

"Yeah, Feds never knew Zay had this place. It's where the bitch Terry lives. You know that's Zay's ho, but she got a kid by Gangsta. If we can snatch her up — or better yet, get the kid — then we good. Fuck around and run into Gangsta, and that'll be perfect," Step boasted while Monkey just listened, still searching the large home for a way in but seeing nothing at all, no way to get in without being seen.

"So how we 'posed to get in this place?" Monkey pulled a Newport out to smoke. He needed the smoke bad. He was still in shock about what happened to Jay. He didn't know that once he told Bam that Jay knew Gangsta that Bam would flip. Monkey was only doing what he thought was right in order to get in better with Bam, but it seemed the plan backfired, because Monkey didn't want Jay dead. He was their homeboy, and he was Monkey's older sister's baby daddy. It was a fucked-up situation to be in, plus he put his self at fault, because he was the nigga who told Bam Gangsta showed up. "I don't see no way."

Step kept looking. "I guess we lay 'bout an hour or two and see if any traffic come through," Step said.

"Lay where, Nigga?" Monkey said, noticing every house on the block was gated and far apart. Step cranked up and pulled off the scene and into traffic. Monkey passed him the cigarette. Step said they would post up at the Racetrack gas station where they could watch the street with its heavy activity. He said, "Maybe we will see Terry riding through, or better yet, Gangsta."

The gas station was hardly packed, so Step quickly pulled over by some payphones and the air-pump machine. He passed the Newport back and cracked the tinted windows.

"Bruh, what you think 'bout that shit Bam pulled on Jay? I mean, don't you think the nigga was being over the top with how he did shawty?" Monkey wanted to know Step's thoughts because he trusted him like a brother.

"To be honest, bruh, naw, he did what any boss would have done. Violence is for order, my nigga, and that's just the code of these wicked streets. He meant to make a statement, and he definitely did." Monkey was disagreeing with the shake of his head, then he cut in. "I can dig that, but we been knowing Jay since way back when, my nigga, and we just started rocking with Bam, what, 'bout three months now? Come on, shawty." Monkey thumped the butt of the cigarette out the cracked window and blew a huge cloud of smoke toward the windshield. Step caught on to his partna's sudden attitude.

"Monkey, my nigga, I feel you, but look at how Bam got us living. We can be rich in no time fucking with dude, for real, bruh. Yeah, I know Jay, been knowing him a lot of years, and he a good nigga, but this game you lose some, you win some. And right now we winning, shawty." Step had his mind made up. It was all about the money, and nothing else mattered to him. Just a couple months ago he didn't have a pot to piss in and no window to throw it out of, and then they ran across Bam, who instantly showed them love by dropping weight on their petty grind. Step was with Bam. *Monkey needs to get with the program before it's too late,* Step thought.

"Man, I'm just saying, you never can tell with this nigga. You don't know if he gon' flip or not. I'm just speaking the facts, bruh, that's it," Monkey stressed, because he saw where this conversation was headed with his childhood friend. Step could be very difficult at times and was almost always stubborn. He was stuck in his ways, as they said. Monkey had dealt with him because they were raised on the same block, went to the same schools, and fucked hos together. He had true love for Step, but Monkey was never the fool.

"I'm with the winning team, shawty. Let that shit go, 'cause Jay gone, my nigga. It is what it is," Step replied, looking at his partner in crime, then added, "We just got a fresh hundred pounds in that we ain't pay a dime for. If we can pull this move here off, I know this nigga Bam will fuck with us heavy, my nigga. Just ride with me. I got us." Step started fumbling with the radio. Monkey looked at him sideways, then replied while pulling out some weed.

"You right, bruh," was the last thing Monkey said. He began rolling the blunt while watching the streets. He didn't want to miss nothing or nobody. He still wasn't feeling Bam, and now he started feeling some type of way about Step, but he would keep that to his self.

Chapter 7

Gangsta

He was looking out the window, lost in deep thought as the SUV rental cruised down the Miami streets, headed to the condo Loco had arranged for them. The sunlight was bright because it was early and beautiful. It was one of them humble mornings when not a lot of people was out. The regular nine-to-five workers were coming and going, the hustlers and all-day petty criminals were among those that walked the streets, but mostly everyone was in the comfort of their beds, dream-chasing.

Today Gangsta felt free — hurt, but free — from the situation with the cops. He felt different being in Miami, unwanted with no pressure. He just prayed Bam's babymama was indeed down here. Gangsta needed Kash out badly. He missed his brother from another mother and knew that if Kash was out, shit would be better. He needed to hear Kash's motivation. He had always known how to get Gangsta on track. Even in an emotional state, Gangsta knew Kash would know what to do in a situation like this. While driving from Georgia, he got a call from Loco saying some of his people found where Bam was located. He was in Mount Zion in a mini-mansion, but the Feds were watching his home from the outside. Gangsta wanted badly to turn around and head back to Atlanta, but he knew that would be a foolish idea, because the last people he wanted to see were the police. Gangsta wanted to stay as far away from the cops as possible. He would deal with the cops face-to-face once he got Bam, but until then he had to remain low key and move swiftly.

It took a twenty-minute drive for them to reach the condo from the highway. The condo was laid when they arrived. It was laced with some of the best furniture, and everything was there for their comfort. Longo tossed the bag of guns on the sofa and went into the kitchen, holding a folder. Jeter closed the door and set the alarm. Gangsta pulled out his phone. He called his mother.

The phone rang a few times and she picked up.

"Son."

"Ma, what's up? Where y'all at?"

"We're safe, at your aunt's house. How about you, though? Are you ok? How is your head feeling?"

"I'm good, ma. What's up with Ne-Ne?" Gangsta asked. "She good?"

"Yes, as a matter of fact, I just got off the phone with her. She's in a room with a phone line now. She is healing, and lord, cranky! But that's Ne-Ne for you," his mother said, and Gangsta liked what he heard, but was afraid to ask the next question. It was an answer he wanted, but was scared to know, because his hope said this, but his heart said different.

"And my son? Any good news?"

There was a pause so silent it seemed like the both of them stopped breathing. Gangsta's insides turned and his eyes closed when he heard his mother's voice begin to crack as she spoke.

"Baby, nothing has changed. I wish it would, but it's not looking good. Doctors said it's no chance, Gary."

Those words crushed him. No real man could swallow that pill, could take that news in stride. It would break the hardest man down just as it was doing Gangsta.

"Ok, ma, give me Nya's number. Is she asleep?" Gangsta quickly changed the subject because he was breaking on the inside, and if it wasn't good news, then he didn't care to hear it.

Once he got Ne-Ne's number, he wasted no time calling her privately. It rang what seemed like a thousand times before her voice came through the speakers, irritated.

"Hello?"

"Baby, what's up?" Gangsta said, which caught Ne-Ne off guard. She closed her eyes at the sound of his voice.

"Gary"

"Yes, listen—"

"Our son is dying," she cut him off. She instantly broke down crying.

That took Gangsta by surprise, so many different emotions rushing out of her. Even though Ne-Ne was acting stubborn to everyone, she was scared and hurt. This wasn't her type of lifestyle. She had never been through any of what Gangsta had going on. Ne-Ne was crying so hard that Gangsta said nothing. He just listened to her cry her heart out, heartbroken himself, but he didn't want to show her he we losing it. He wanted to show her strength.

"Gary, you didn't protect us. You jeopardized us for them fuckin' streets, and now my son has a twenty percent chance of living 'cause the choices you made. You didn't protect us. You brought that shit right to our doorstep, Gary. Why?" Ne-Ne cried harder.

"Baby, listen, it's not ev—"

"No, you listen," she cut him off. "The hospital is trying—"

"Don't pull the plug, no matter what they say," Gangsta cut her back off.

"Oh, trust and believe I won't." Ne-Ne was still crying. "Insurance won't hold up, though, and—"

"Nya," Gangsta said as humble as possible. He was in love still with her and didn't like to see her like this.

"What, Gary?"

"Don't worry 'bout no money for my son. Just get better and pray, baby, ok? I love you, ok?"

"Bye, Gary."

"Nya?" Gangsta spoke, but there was nobody one the line. She was gone, and he couldn't say he blamed her, but right now wasn't the time for them to be falling apart. She was supposed to be his number one fan, because when a person's girl, wife, family believe in them, it makes them go harder. It gives them reasons, and that's what he longed to have from the woman he was in love with.

Gangsta tossed his phone over on the sofa next to the bag of guns. He went into the kitchen where Longo was looking over a printout of Bam's babymama's mom's house. There was also a map and a host of pictures sprawled out on the countertop. Gangsta took a seat on the stool next to him.

"Ok, so what are we looking at?" He was truly interested.

"Everything, my friend. A route to get in and out. A time to check every street for a hidden camera. We must study the traffic, the cops. Everybody and everything should work together if we plan to pull this off without being noticed down here. The last thing Loco wanted was bad blood between his people in Miami," Longo spoke, not taking his eyes from the paperwork he had prepared.

"Ok, so just let me know when you ready to go handle this issue. I need to get me a lil' mental rest, feel me?" He patted Longo's shoulder while getting to his feet.

"Hey, way?" Longo caught him before he left the kitchen.

"What's up, way?" Gangsta stopped and turned his attention back to the Mexican.

"Loco really likes you, has vouched for you. You know, that's the reason we are here with you. Thus far, I like you too, way. You're smart and humble with your shit, amigo. After this ordeal is over, you will become a very rich man with power, and my friend, you deserve it." Gangsta only looked at Longo, who turned away first, looking back over his handout.

"'Preciate it, way. Real talk, brother."

Gangsta grabbed his phone en route to finding a room with a bed. He lay across it and dialed a number.

"Hello," she answered.

"Ebony, what's going on?"

There was a pause on the other end, then Gangsta heard her sitting up before she spoke. "Who is this?"

"It's Gangsta."

"Ok, I figured that. How are you holding up?" she asked, concerned because he was like a brother to her and was an uncle to her kids.

"I'm good, Sis, just tore up 'bout my son, you know."

"Yes, I'm following the case now. I just hate how the media is making Ne-Ne out to be an unfit mother because she refuses to remove your son from life support. And charging you with murder instead of self defense is crazy." Even though Ebony was a homicide detective, she would never turn on her brother. She was more loyal to her love than her job.

"Yeah, shit is crazy, and the world is against me right now, but not for long. Once I handle my business, I got a plan. So how are the kids? Have you heard from Kash?"

"The kids are great, and I looked Kash up. He's on maximum security at Jackson State Prison. I wrote him, but haven't got a reply," Ebony shot back.

"Cool. So listen, talk to Kash's mom and pops about getting him another lawyer so he can withdraw his guilty plea. He gotta go through some different courts, but it can happen. Also, I need you to check and see exactly what they got on me." Gangsta had something up his sleeve.

"I will make the call to Kash's parents, but you know my district is Cobb County. Well, I got a best friend at front desk in Atlanta, so yeah, I got you, bruh."

"Bet that, Sis. I'ma keep in touch," Gangsta replied, and he got off the phone.

He got up off the bed and searched the room until he found what he was looking for. Once he got the book, Gangsta opened it to the far back until he found Hebrews eleven and read the entire scripture. He read slowly so he could take in exactly what the verses were saying. Gangsta was broken down, and he needed the faith of some of those he was reading about. Tears slowly rolled from Gangsta's eyes as thoughts of Junior wouldn't leave his mind, plus Ne-Ne being stubborn wasn't helping at all. It crushed his insides not to have her love anymore, and for her to say the things she said about him. No matter what, Gangsta felt like they should come together, rather than being apart. They needed to be strong for their son.

Gangsta closed the Bible and got down on his knees. The only person who could help him now was God, so that's who he was going to.

God, you said all I need is the faith, all I have to do is ask and it would be given to me. Lord, my son is lying in a hospital bed eighty percent dead, twenty percent living, and his mother hates my guts. God, I ask you to fix this.

Tears fell rapidly down his face now.

God, I know I'm no saint, and in your book my sins are great, but Junior, he's just a kid. Lord, please spare my son. God, please heal my son with a miracle, because he deserves a shot at life. He's only two. God, please hear my cry, and I got faith that you do hear me and he will be healed. God, he's barely even two yet. His sins are not sins. He's innocent, God. I'm begging you.

Gangsta broke down harder than he ever had. His emotions had gotten the best of him as the cries rushed out of him. He was helpless, didn't know what to do. Just the mere thought was eating up his insides. He did not want his son to die. He could not bury him.

God, please spare my son, Nya, my daughter, and mom and auntie. Please protect them all, Lord. God, please lighten the heart of Nya. God, I need her. Lord, I pray and ask all these things in Jesus' name. Amen.

Gangsta got up and wiped his face with his shirt. He lay across the bed, taking a deep breath and closing his eyes. His mind was in overtime. Something had to give, and fast.

***

Monkey

They finally left Racetrack after being there three hours. Monkey had to talk Step into driving to the Westside where Gangsta was from. Monkey stressed that it was better than just sitting in College Park with little chance of finding anybody linked to Gangsta. Monkey knew a couple folks on the Westside who would side with him before they would with Gangsta, so he decided to take a trip over after convincing Step. Once they made it to Hollywood Road, Monkey ran into a smoker he knew named Randy, who was willing to help. They rode to Do Drop In, a hood store. Step sent the dude Randy inside to get blunts and sodas. When he was out of the car, Monkey looked over to Step.

"Did that pack make it to the spot?" Monkey asked about the new shipment of loud.

"Yeah, I told you that already, bruh. But look, I'm focused on this move, my nigga, when we knock Gangsta off," Step replied, rubbing both his hands together with a slick smile on his face.

Monkey ignored his comment. While texting on his phone, he stated, "I got two niggas want twenty apiece."

"Them niggas can wait. We got bigger fish to fry."

"Bruh, what the fuck we look like, turning down a forty-pound jump off? Let's get this money, then we lurk the city," Monkey spoke, aggravated.

Step didn't respond because Randy was walking back to the car. They pulled off when he was inside. Monkey clipped his phone to the sun visor. They rode up Hollywood Road listening to Velt, an un-signed rapper that was hot in the streets, then down Johnson Road, but saw nobody worth talking to. Monkey was getting more aggravated, because Step's mind was not on the money.

"Say, bruh, I'm finna make the play for them forty," Monkey said out of nowhere.

"Bruh, get yo' mind off that, my nigga. We trying to handle business. You need to stay focused," Step said back, now looking at Monkey.

"Naw, nigga, you need to get focused. I just got another play to the phone, and we riding around chasing a ghost. I guess that's more important than the next day re-up," Monkey shot back. He was heated. Step turned in his seat.

"You know I want the money, but I want the position I know we gon' get if we pull this off," Step boasted. He knew Monkey was right, but his greed for more wouldn't let him admit it, so he continued to make up excuses. Monkey shook his head.

"Shawty, this Nigga is on the run for triple homicide. We out here hunting for this nigga like we the police. We have turned into some overnight hitmen, missing out on stupid racks. We got plenty of shooters and niggas that will die for us, but this, what we doing here, will put us out there." Monkey was tired of explaining the importance of their money. Step was being stupid right now, and Monkey wasn't with it. "Ride over to Baker Road, bruh. My lil' cousin probably know some shit," was the last thing Monkey said. He was pissed, and Step knew it, but he didn't care, as always.

"You say Baker Road?" asked Step sarcastically.

"Yeah."

It didn't take long for them to get there from Johnson Road. Step was rapping some of the lyrics of Velt as it pumped through the speakers.

Work like temp services. Fans like Oprah, die hard fans in my hood is the smokers. I don't call them Jack boys, I call them jokers. Same niggas get locked up, bitch out, and fold up.

When they made it to Baker Road, Monkey directed him to a red brick house with a couple cars out front and a few dudes sitting in the driveway, drinking, smoking, and jamming to the radio of a car. Almost everybody's face lit up when Monkey jumped out of the ride.

He embraced two of the four dudes as Step watched, along with Randy.

"I need a favor, Unc," Monkey said to a heavyset, tall, light-skinned man. He had a serious look on his face.

"What's up, Nephew? Let's talk. Come on." His uncle walked off from the group in the driveway and into the house that was neatly decorated just like a old school would do. Monkey turned around to face his uncle once they were solo inside the crib.

"Them niggas in the car I'm finna kill. I need you to help me pull this off, though, and I'ma fuck with you big on this drop I got."

When Monkey said what he said, his uncle just looked at him dumbfounded, then shook his head. "Correct me if I'm wrong, but isn't that your ace in the driver's seat out there?"

Monkey walked closer and said through gritted teeth, "Uncle. this nigga is 'bout to get us killed, or better yet, a life sentence. He on some more shit. Trust me, he got to go."

His uncle saw in Monkey's face that he wasn't joking. "So you want me to catch the life sentence with you?" his uncle laughed.

"Fuck no. That's why I asked you to help me, 'cause I know you good at this shit. But either way, it's gonna happen, Unc." Monkey had his mind made up already.

"I feel you, Nephew, but I can't take that chance. I'm too old for another jail cell, homie. Take them niggas right there on Church Street and handle yo' business and get back here. I will get you, home." His uncle was a known killer back in his days. He did twenty years for murder, and he wasn't willing to do another day, but he did give his nephew some pointers.

"Cool, Unc." Monkey walked back outside after they dapped each other up. He threw up the deuce to the other three guys in the driveway and jumped into the car. He looked over at Step. "Unc said Gangsta's auntie stay on Church Street, bruh, right 'round the corner," Monkey lied, closing the door.

Jerry Jackson

Chapter 8

Gangsta

Longo woke him up with a plate of food and something to drink. Gangsta sat up, still sleepy from his power nap, feeling a sharp pain run through his chest. He rubbed it before he took the food from the Mexican. "'Preciate it, way."

"No problem. We pull out in thirty minutes, so get your stuff together," Longo said and left the room, leaving Gangsta to his meal. He rubbed his chest one more time, then picked up the phone. He had no missed calls. He had been asleep a few hours, and he felt a lil' better. It didn't take him long to smash the food and get up. Jeter and Longo were eating when he made it to the living room. There were a few guns laid out on the table. Both Longo and Jeter wore all black, both had masks rolled on top of their heads. Longo tossed Gangsta one and a pair of gloves. Gangsta noticed all the guns had silencers on them.

"You ready, way?"

"Fuckin' right. I'm ready to get back to the city and handle the big business," Gangsta replied while rolling the mask on top of his head.

"Let's roll." Jeter stood up.

Longo passed everybody two guns before saying, "One is for backup."

Gangsta didn't protest. He just took them and they all headed out the door.

Bam's babymama was located in a very nice area in Miami on South Miami Avenue. It took them an hour's drive and two blunts to get there. It was almost 7:00 p.m., so the streets were fairly empty and quiet. Jeter was driving. He parked across the street from the brown brick home that sat twenty feet from the road. No gate surrounded the nice looking house. The three of them sat in silence.

Longo was reading from some notes, then looking at his watch. Gangsta held one of the P9 Rugars tightly in his palm, ready to get shit popping.

"What's the plan, Longo," Jeter asked.

"A knock warrant. We have only ten minutes to handle the business. We rush in, we kill the entire house, we back out, and we leave."

"No kids, way. I'm not killing no kids," Gangsta spoke.

"Loco say everything dies. He don't want not one witness," Longo said over his shoulder and opened the door, leaving Gangsta no reply. He and Jeter followed Longo as he smoothly walked across the street.

"Come on, way," Jeter spoke to Gangsta, leading him around the side of the house while Longo took the other way. Jeter found a door under the carport that led into the house. They waited until Longo met up with them before Jeter tried the doorknob, and it turned, cracking the door. It took them inside a kitchen. Longo put one finger over his lips, then pointed down to a sleeping dog. Longo aimed the P9 and pulled the trigga. It sounded like wind as the bullet tore through the dog's skull, blood beginning to pool from under him.

"No witnesses, way."

They all went their separate ways. Longo and Gangsta headed upstairs as Jeter went to find the living room. The first room Gangsta entered held a female who had to be Bam's babymama. She looked up when Gangsta entered the room, his gun aimed at her face. Goldie still tried to run to the closet, but he was on her with lighting speed.

"Bitch, you better chill." Gangsta pressed the gun to the side of her face. He looked up and noticed a little girl no more than four years old standing at the foot of the bed. She was very pretty with a fresh bowtie hairdo.

"Please don't hurt my child," Goldie mumbled with pleading eyes.

"Don't give me a reason. How many kids are in this house?" Gangsta asked, pulling out some cuffs.

"My son is in the bathroom," she spoke fearfully, shaking like she just came in from the rain in the winter.

He heard a scream from the next room over, then quickly nothing. Gangsta knew someone just lost their life. He had to move fast. He quickly cuffed Goldie from behind. There was rumbling downstairs, which made Goldie start crying.

"Bitch, where is your phone?" Gangsta said with the gun aimed at her face. The girl's shaky head pointed to the phone laying next to her iPad. Gangsta took it. "What's your name?"

"I'm— I-I'm— My name is Goldie. Please don't kill m—"

Her words were abruptly stopped when the bullet connected with her cheekbone, spraying the wall with blood. The little girl didn't stir. Gangsta looked down at her, and with a second thought, he put the gun on his hip. He got the phone and took a picture of Goldie. He then bent down to the little girl.

"I'm 'bout to hide you in the closet so you will not be hurt, ok?" He was hoping the little girl understood him, because if Longo saw her, she was as good as dead. He put her in the closet quickly, walking out of the room. He and Longo met up in the hallway, both heading to the last room. When they made it, there was a younger female who looked like a college student. She jumped up when Gangsta hit the lights and she found two men in her room. She was just about to scream, but Longo was already busting his shots to her stomach and chest area. Her body hit the ground, jerked a bit, then life left it. Gangsta looked at Longo, then they both walked off.

Longo was about to check the bathroom, so Gangsta beat him to the punch. He quickly walked in and there was a little boy. He and Gangsta locked eyes, then Gangsta left, going back downstairs where Jeter was waiting on them. It was a total wreck in the living room. Two bodies of older females lay bloody on the carpet. Gangsta walked over them toward the door. They all slipped out of the house and quickly back to the car. Longo cranked up and pulled off down South Miami Avenue.

No one spoke as the car sped up the block, making a couple turns, then back to the highway. Non-stop, they were headed back to Georgia.

Gangsta pulled his phone out, then pulled the girl's phone out. He scrolled through her call log and saw the last number that called her. It had to be Bam, he thought. He dialed it back. The phone rang a few times and rolled over to voicemail. He probably would've hung up if Bam answered. Gangsta smiled when he heard Bam's voice. He then went through her text messages to see what they had been talking about, but saw nothing of importance. Gangsta was feeling like he was making progress. He knew Bam would be sick once he found out he couldn't hide. Gangsta could've played really dirty and killed the kids, but he didn't have the nuts because the kids didn't have anything to do with what Bam had going on, so he spared them like he would want a man to spare his kids. And even though the man didn't spare his son, Gangsta's heart still couldn't pull a trigger on a kid, no matter what.

"Way," Longo broke his train of thought, making him look up to the front seat.

"What's hap', way?"

"No witnesses, right?" Longo asked.

"Yeah, no witnesses, way," Gangsta replied, but then wondered why Longo asked that. Could it be he saw it in Gangsta's eyes that he was hiding something? However it went, Gangsta didn't give two fucks. His son was on life support from a heartless nigga, and that was somebody he wasn't. Right then and there in the car, Gangsta silently made a vow to never take another man's life once he found and killed Bam. Even though he was street, he still had some form of a heart, and it seemed crazy because he killed without thought at times.

Gangsta knew he was changing because he was a father now, and he wasn't just living for himself anymore. He had people to raise. They smoked four blunts before Longo decided to stop for something to eat right outside of Miami. Gangsta used that time to call Ne-Ne, just to check up on her.

She picked up. "Hello?"

"Baby, how you feeling?" he asked.

"What's up, Gary?"

"Nya, I need you in my corner, baby, not being hateful. Because you my strength, baby girl. You always have been. Any word on Junior yet?" he needed to know.

"Same status. He's being moved to Grady tomorrow, and I'm being released, but I'm not leaving his side. I spoke with a specialist about surgery on Junior. He said it's worth a try, since I don't want to give up, but the chance of him making it is none. Nobody ever has come back from being brain dead. This is what the doctor said," Ne-Ne told him.

Gangsta just took in everything he was hearing, then he said, "Nya, I love you, baby girl. God got us. Let him do the surgery. I'm on my way back to Atlanta. I wanna see you."

"Gary I don't wanna see you right now. I'm not about to lie and say I do. I want my son to wake up. That's what I want, so give me that."

"I am, Nya."

"*I can't fuckin' tell,*" she yelled through the phone. Gangsta had to move it from his ear. "I'm starting to hate you, Gary."

Ne-Ne was breaking down again. Gangsta knew she was hurt, though her words were crushing him. If she only knew how he felt, maybe she would be more considerate of her words, but she was in a blind rage right now.

"I'ma call you tomorrow on my mom's phone." He just hung up in her face. He was starting to become pissed off as well, and he was desperately trying not to blow up on her, because he knew the situation and understood.

"Roll up one more, way." Gangsta tossed Jeter the loud he needed to blow one.

***

Monkey

Step pulled up on Church Street and rode at a slow pace until Monkey told him to stop in front of one of the houses. They both looked hard in the same direction of the house. As Step was looking, Monkey eased his hand around the butt of his gun. His finger eased around the trigga. His heart rate sped up in his chest at the thought of what he was about to do. Could he truly take his friend's life just out of nowhere? Monkey wasn't that type of guy. He wasn't pussy, but killing wasn't natural. Once he made a move, there was no turning back. He knew that. Step was his ace since knee high. It wasn't easy taking his life, but if he didn't, then the ending wasn't gonna be pretty for them both. Something had to be done, because Step had flipped.

Monkey already had a plan mapped out to cross out Bam by linking up with Gangsta. He would deliver Bam right to Gangsta on a silver platter. Plus he would get to keep the hundred pounds of loud and bank on Gangsta being the plug, as he said he would. With one quick motion, the gun raised up. At the same time, Step was turning back toward Monkey. The gun exploded, knocking blood and brain all over the driver's side window. Monkey turned around to a shocked Randy in the back. He aimed the gun and let off two more shots, both striking his face, slumping him. Monkey wiped everything down before he jumped out of the whip and took off running toward his uncle's house. When Monkey made it up the street, his uncle and crew were already getting their stuff together, ready to leave. Monkey, breathing heavily, nodded to his uncle, who directed him to his truck.

"Give me a second. Let me lock up this house." His uncle moved fast as his buddies were pulling out. Nobody wanted to be a part of this. Every last one of them had been to prison before, and it was no more going back. They didn't care what the next man did, it was just certain shit they were no longer willing to do. Unc made it to the truck and quickly pulled off down Baker Road, headed to I-20. Monkey started feeling bad when they got on the highway, because Step had always been his right hand. It was gonna be nearly impossible to look Step's mom in the face after knowing he was the one who killed her son. It was done already, ain't no taking it back, so he must move on to the next mission in life.

Monkey had his uncle drop him off at the spot so he could check the trap.

"You good, nephew?" he asked Monkey when they posted in the driveway. Monkey had one foot in, one foot out of the car, his gun laid cross his lap. He waved a guy over from the porch of the trap house, then he looked at his uncle.

"Yeah, I'm good, Unc. I'ma look out for you, too, when I get this shit situated." They dapped each other up as Monkey got out to meet the guy who looked like a junkie.

"What's up, Monkey?"

"Where is Pam?" They walked toward the house as his uncle pulled off. The junkie looked over his shoulder, then back to Monkey.

"Her and Mack in there. Where is your shadow? When I see you, I see him," the junkie asked about Step, but Monkey ignored him, going into the house that smelled like loud weed. The living room was crowded with niggas standing around, holding choppers, standing guard. Pam and Mack were in the back room. Monkey walked into it after talking with a few of the shooters they had standing around.

Jerry Jackson

"Glad you here. This shit gon' take more than a day to break up in pounds, it's to compressed," Mack said once he saw Monkey. Mack was their most loyal worker, and Pam was family through years of hanging around. She was the hood lil' freak for many years, plus she was loyal and down.

"So what you saying, we need more days?" Monkey asked while touching one of the bails of loud.

"At least one more," Pam said as sweat dripped from her face.

"I tell you what, go pick two of them shooters to help speed up the process, 'cause this shit got to be ready to move tomorrow. Pam, I need your ride and your presence. Grab your strap. Mack, make sure shit on point."

"Say no mo'. Whe' Step ass at?" Mack asked.

"Step resting, bruh. Hit me when you get half pound up," Monkey replied, leaving the room. Pam was beside him.

Pam drove a silver BMW SUV tricked out. Monkey jumped in the driver's seat, sinking into the leather. He adjusted the seat for his comfort, then pulled off.

"Everything good, ain't it?" Pam asked, because she could tell by his demeanor that it wasn't, that there was something going on.

Monkey sped down the street. Without looking at her, he said, "I just murked Step."

Chapter 9

Bam

Trina rode nested under him as the Benz truck cruised through Buckhead after dodging the Feds the night before. A Tahoe in the front and a Tahoe in the back protected Bam as he puffed on some of the best loud he could find. One of his arms draped over Trina's shoulders, his hand resting on the side of her bubble booty. He passed her the blunt while taking in the view of Buckhead: condos and storefronts. He had a beautiful surprise for Trina that would blow her mind. Even though Bam was a cold-blooded killer, he still had some affection in him and didn't mind showing it. His babymama Goldie was the first lady. She was the one female that was close to him, that pushed his button, and that knew him like a book, so she saw more of the softer side of him with his kids. Goldie was the one he was in love with. Trina was next in line, because he was crazy about her, too. They just didn't have history like him and Goldie.

The big-body Benz pulled up to the Cheesecake Factory, which brightened Trina's face. Bam smiled, knowing the effect he had on her. She passed the blunt back to him, then sat up.

"Daddy, you know this my spot, right?" Trina happily said.

Bam sat up also. He patted her thigh before saying, "So now you know I listen, shorty."

They stepped out of the Benz, both decked out in Gucci from the neck down. Bam was iced out, blinding those that watched him. Everywhere Bam went, he was the life of the party. Everyone flocked to him when he would step out, because Bam partied like a rock star. The FBI gave him a pass, and since he was already exposed, he flaunted his wealth.

Bam had plans to leave Georgia once court was over with. He would just work with Monkey and Step while Trina oversaw the entire operation. Trina had the heart, plus she took instructions well enough to handle two niggas in Atlanta. Bam knew he needed to fall back out of the Feds' eye, but money still have to be made, so he planned to setup shop in Texas, a place he hadn't put his stamp down in yet.

Once inside the Cheesecake Factory, they were seated. Trina had a beautiful smile painted on her face, looking across to the guy she was in love with. Bam was looking at the menu as the waiter approached, placing two wine glasses on the table and a card. Trina eyed the card, but said nothing while Bam ordered their food.

"Daddy, I'm loving this. I'm loving you." She couldn't hold it in any longer.

"Yo, I'm glad you are, ma." Bam picked the card up. "I got some major plans for you, baby girl."

"Really?" Trina gave him a devilish look. Her pussy automatically started getting moist as thoughts of them fucking ran through her mind.

"Get your mind out the gutter, shorty. I'm talking about some money, baby. Yo, it will be plenty fucking later. Right now, ma, we gots to build a foundation that nobody can break up and knock down," Bam said, then opened the card. It was a card key and instructions on a sticky note. He pushed it across the table toward her. Trina's eyes went down to the small writing. She read the note, then looked back across to Bam.

"I'm with you, Daddy," was the only thing she said, taking the card key as Bam kept the note. He ripped it at the table.

"That's what I need to know, shorty. That's love."

Shortly after they talked, their food arrived, and neither Bam nor Trina played with the plates.

They left the restaurant and hit the World Bar for a few more drinks. It wasn't that packed, so they sat at the bar and ordered shots. On the third round, Trina had gotten loose and started to dance in her seat.

"Daddy, come cut one wit' me." She stood from her seat, ready to dance.

"I'm good, shorty." Bam balled his face up.

"Please, Daddy," Trina begged, but Bam wasn't moved at all.

"No, baby girl. I'm not the dancing type. Now, you can go out there and stunt if you choose. You know I'm right here and won't nobody fuck with you, ma," Bam assured her.

"Ok, but still, I want to dance with you, though." Trina tried desperately to convince him, but Bam was a killer, not no dancer. He sold drugs for a living, not for nothing else.

"What'd I say, shorty?" Bam's voice became serious, which made Trina straightened up.

"Ok, Daddy, then just watch me put on for you." She walked to the dance floor, then looked over her shoulder to see if Bam was watching. She noticed his eyes were glued to her, so she blew him a kiss and dropped her fat booty to the floor, then brought it up, making it clap, stealing almost everyone's attention in the bar. Bam just smiled at her while downing another shot.

He looked at his phone and saw Monkey and Step hadn't called to confirm they received the hundred pounds he sent, nor had he gotten a call about progress on Gangsta or his family.

Trina put both her hands on her knees and bounced her ass so hard her Gucci dress rolled up to her back. Guys started to migrate over that weren't already there. It was like all niggas when they had liquor in them — they lost all control. One dude with dreads stepped out of the circle that formed around her. He reached out and grabbed a handful of booty. He squeezed it, making Trina stop dancing. She spun around on him, looked him up and down before walking up on him. Grabbing a handful of dick and balls, she squeezed with all her might, making the dude double over in pain. He somehow pushed out of her grip and slapped the taste out of her mouth.

"Bitch—"

"Yo, son." Bam was on his feet in no time. The dude spun around to a fist and two bows to the face. "Nigga, is you nuts?" Bam said, taking a step back to allow the dude to get right, but to no avail. He could not get his feet to work together. The crowd moved back with a lot of mumbles as security approached, walking up on Bam.

"Calm down, sir." One of the bouncers held his hand out. By then two of Bam's bodyguards walked up on security, stepping in their path. Trina was cranked now and already was half drunk. She started charging at the already dazed dude, but Bam held her with one arm while speaking to security.

"Yo, look, I'm the oppressed. I don't have the problem. Son do." Then Bam pointed to the guy he dropped.

"That motherfucker grabbed my pussy and would not let my shit go," Trina lied, but the way she was acting, everybody in the bar believed her, even the ones who saw the whole thing.

"Ok, cool. Uh, take your girl and y'all just dip," the security guard said, looking at Trina.

The other guard stepped in. "Or you can press charges, but buddy here might go to jail then." He pointed to Bam, then to the dude, raising his eyebrow. Bam and Trina quickly got the picture and they eased up out of the establishment

"Daddy, get me the fuck out of Buckhead." Trina slammed the Benz's door.

Bam looked at her like she was stupid before he replied, "Yo, calm down, shorty. Dead that shit, ma. See, you need to learn how to control your temper in order to run shit. You will be seeing these same people daily while I'm away, and I do not need for these folks to see you the wrong way."

"I'm just saying, Daddy, didn't you see this nigga trying me like I'm some action or something? Fuck I look like?"

"Yo, but that shit over, ma. But yo' emotions still out of sync. You got to learn control, baby. I need you to."

"You right, Daddy." Trina was still hot and he knew it. She was young, but she was ready, and that was something he liked. She was pure gangsta at heart. He just needed her to find the control button. The Benz pulled up to some of the most expensive condos in Buckhead, which caught her attention. Bam led the way through the lobby to the elevator.

He held Trina from behind and whispered in her ear, "I love you, ma, just know that. See, baby, I'm about to put the world at your feet, but you got to help me help you by toning down that fire in your heart. There's a time and place for violence, ma. Once you get this in you, then you helping me."

He turned her around in his arms as the elevator doors opened. He softly kissed her lips, and she kissed him back. When they got to the door, Bam told her to use the card key. Entering the condo, Trina lost her breath when she saw how lavishly it was laid out.

"This you, shorty. Since you 'bout to oversee Georgia, I want you to do it in style. It would've been a house, but you just twenty-four, and the Feds is lurking. They will be at your doorstep fast, but this low key, ma."

"Daddy, I love it!" The excitement was in her every word as she walked around the entire condo.

Bam told his bodyguards that he and Trina were good, giving them the remainder of the day off. When Trina made it back up front, they were gone and Bam was on the futon, rolling a blunt to smoke.

"Daddy, you the shit," she said.

"Oh yeah?"

"Daddy, yes!"

Bam lit the blunt up, then leaned back. He hit it two hard times and blew smoke toward her.

"So, you appreciate this?" Bam waved his hands.

"Everything you ever did for me I appreciate." Trina meant those words.

"Show me how much, ma. Come show me how much."

Trina smiled and led Bam to the bed by one hand. She turned him around and softly pushed his chest. Bam sat back on the edge of the bed, blunt between his fingers, with a smirk on his face. Trina stripped out of her Gucci and stood before him naked. She had a banging body with almost perfect breasts. With his free hand, Bam ran a trail from her chest down to her shaved pussy with a butterfly piercing in its lips. Bam hit the blunt again, then kissed her stomach before standing to his feet. Trina pulled his shirt over his head, then unfasten the Gucci belt holding his pants up. She unbuttoned his jeans and reached into his boxer shorts, pulling his hardness out. Trina kissed his chest, his stomach, his hipbone, and finally his dick, up and down it. Bam sat back down and enjoyed the pleasure Trina delivered as she sucked him good and slow, also taking his balls into her mouth.

"Let me feel that throat, ma," Bam urged her on, and she complied with a moan. Trina looked at his facial expression to see if she was doing a good job, and by the way his eyes were shut tight, she knew her oral skills were working. Trina let Bam slide in and out of her throat, almost making her gag, but somehow she managed to control it and allowed Bam to cum in her mouth. Not missing a drop of him, Trina happily swallowed his sperm. With his dick still hard as ever, Bam entered her with two long strokes and a deep push inside her warm, wet pussy. Trina opened her legs wide and wrapped her arms around his neck as he went to work on her insides.

***

Monkey

"You what?" Pam was caught off guard with his statement. Wasn't no way in God's green earth she heard him correctly. Her ears had to be playing tricks on her. "What did you say?" She had to hear him again. This couldn't be true.

Monkey gripped the wheel, then let it go and slapped his palm down on it hard, making Pam think he was about to push the steering wheel in. "I fuck 'round and had to take bruh out. He was doing too much, Pam, for real. This nigga Bam had him brainwashed. He wasn't the same Step we knew. He was 'bout to bring us down, real talk. He was 'bout to get us killed or locked up, so I took him out." It was hard for Monkey to admit, but he did, and telling the truth sounded and felt better. But it bothered him to kill his friend. It wasn't the normal shit they did in the hood. It was an act of disloyalty to take a partna's life, or any life of them that trusted the killer.

"Damn, Monkey. What the fuck, man? What the hell happened?" Pam wanted to know.

"Man, Step was running behind this nigga Gangsta, trying to knock him off instead of getting to the money. He claimed to want a better position fuckin' with our new connect, and killing this dude Gangsta was the key." Monkey was furious.

"And what's wrong with that? Isn't this what y'all wanted?" Pam asked. Monkey shook his head.

"It's a long story. Let's just say the connect is a snake, plus Gangsta promised us better deals, better dope. The thing is we don't know Gangsta, and we hardly know Bam, but this nigga ain't right. The true question is do this nigga Gangsta got the product he boast to have? It's like this," Monkey paused, then continued. "Bam wants him dead, and Gangsta wants the same, and we caught up in the middle of this shit. I did what's best — at least that's what I thought."

"So what's the plan?" replied Pam. Monkey thought about it for a second. He looked out to the road.

"The plan is to side with Gangsta and turn this nigga Bam over to Gangsta the nasty way. We got to find him fast, though, before word get out that Step is dead. I'ma keep the whole hundred pounds. I'm not giving this sucka a penny, so with him dead, I don't got to duck and hide," Monkey replied

"Just call the nigga Gangsta then," said Pam.

"He never gave me or step his info. He was too paranoid, but I know some personal people who know of him and his most trusted hang out. I was thinking about riding through to see if I could bump heads with one of the people I know."

Monkey lit up a cigarette. His nerves were becoming very bad. Time wasn't on his side. He didn't really wanna be doing this. He'd much rather be getting to the paperwork, but Step fucked everything up, going at the entire situation wrong. And to make matters worse, he showed no type of sympathy when Jay got killed, so it made him question their trust.

"Well, let's get over there. You know I'm with you and all, but man, Step was family, like a brother. All of us is like family. I know how he could get self-centered at times. I'm just in a state of shock right now, that's all, but I'm with you, Monkey." Pam also lit up a cigarette, pulling and inhaling hard.

Chapter 10

Gangsta

He was so glad to make it back to Atlanta without any problems. Loco was there when they arrived with a bright smile on his face.

"Way!"

"What's up, way?" Gangsta smiled also, then gave him some dap.

"Glad to see you back. How you feel?" They shook hands.

"I feel the same, my friend. I will only feel better when Bam's head explodes from his shoulders. I'ma keep it real with you too, way. I can't kill no kids. Yeah, maybe before now, but man my son been shot. I just can't do that. I spared the kids though, way, but they was asleep," Gangsta lied.

Longo jumped to his feet. "So you lied to me, amigo."

"No. I told you no witnesses 'cause I knew the kids was asleep. They tiny babies, like my son, way. I couldn't." Gangsta looked at Loco, hoping he understood where he was coming from.

"But yo' son got shot, right? The shit would have hurt the nigga if you played eye-for-an-eye, my friend," Longo said, walking up and clearly mad that Gangsta lied to him.

"I'm asking God to spare my son. Fuck I look like killing two kids, way? This gon' hurt him right here." Gangsta pulled Bam's babymama's phone out and showed Loco the picture, then he sent it to Bam. He passed it to Longo, who passed it to Jeter.

"I fully understand my friend," Loco said as Melody walked into the living room. She waved at Gangsta, glad to see him. He waved back.

"Off limits, way." Loco patted Gangsta's shoulder.

"Say no mo'."

"My brother don't run me." Melody laughed just a bit.

"I was only teasing, way. My sisters are grown and I trust their judgment, as I trust yours, too. Come have dinner with us. Sit back and relax a lil'," Loco said through a smile.

"I can't, way. I got some business right quick that can't be put off. 'Preciate it though, my friend," Gangsta replied.

"Fine. Well, my father's last day here is tomorrow and I have sold him on your qualities. And he wants to meet you."

"I will be back in a couple hours." Gangsta dapped Loco once more, then Jeter and Longo before heading out the door. Gangsta was feeling almost ok, though his son was the biggest issue he had in his heart. If he could just get God to save Junior, it would be amazing. Gangsta would trade his life for that type of miracle.

Inside the car, he called his mother. She picked up quickly.

"Hello?"

"Ma, what's up?" Gangsta asked.

"Hey, baby. You ok?" Joy was in her voice.

"I'm good, ma. Whe' is y'all?"

"Still at your aunt's. Me and Erica is going to get Ne-Ne later on today, 'cause she's being released. Oh, and hold on. Terry wants to talk to you." His mother put him on hold, and seconds later Terry's voice came through.

"Gary?"

"What's up?"

"Gary, some guy went over to Nikki's house looking for you. He left a number, saying that he got something for you. Roxanne had called me 'bout it. Do you want his number?" she asked.

"Yeah, come on with it. Whe' is my baby?" Gangsta questioned while fumbling with his thoughts. *Who could it be?*

"Keshana is right here under me." Terry gave him the number and put Keshana on the phone for a quick second. He missed his baby girl, and she missed him to the point she didn't want to get off the phone. Gangsta promised to see her soon, then his mother got back on the phone.

"Baby, have you talked to your lawyer yet?" she asked.

"Not yet, ma. What's up?"

"Well, he made the cops drop that warrant. Now they only looking for you for questioning, but if they catch you, they will hold you. Call him, though. I can't remember everything he said."

"Yeah, I'ma get at him. First things first, I'm going to see my son and Ne-Ne. You think the cops down there messing with her?" Gangsta asked his mother, because he wasn't sure if he should, but he had the burning desire to go still, whether wrong or right.

"I don't know, baby, but that's not a good idea to go down there. Gary, you are not thinking clearly, son. The police could be out there looking, and anybody could see you and call it in," his mother pleaded. She was worried

"I'm willing to take my chances, ma. Ne-Ne's acting unlike herself, and I don't need that right now. I need to see Junior now, and it can't wait." Gangsta was determined to get some understanding with Ne-Ne. He wouldn't just sit and wait on her to come to her senses. He had to make her see the clear picture.

"If I'm not mistaken, I think he's gone already, baby. I'm not for sure, though. And why don't you call Ne-Ne before you just go down there? Call and talk with her before you go to popping up. You might scare the life out of her, baby."

Gangsta heard what his mother was saying, but her words went in one ear and fell out the other. He needed to talk to Ne-Ne face-to-face. Nothing would stop him from making that happen.

After Gangsta ended the call, he reached out to Nikki about the dude who left his number. Nikki's baby voice boomed through the speakers.

"Hello?"

"Nikki. What's hap, shawty? Dis Gangsta," he said.

"Gangsta, ok. What's up, bruh? Do you know a nigga named Monkey? 'Cause he pulled up over here with a very pretty female on some humble shit asking where could he find you," Nikki told him.

"What's his name?" Gangsta wanted to know

"Some Nigga named Monkey," she repeated. "What's up, though? Are you ok, bruh?" Nikki's concerned voice asked.

"I'm straight, shawty. I'm finna hit this nigga. I'ma keep you posted," Gangsta said and ended the call. He quickly dialed the number he got from Terry.

"'Lo?"

Gangsta remembered the face to the voice when the dude picked up. "Whoa, this Gangsta. What's hap, bruh?" Gangsta was already expecting these niggas to be brainwashed by Bam, and this nigga was on some bullshit.

"This Monkey, shawty. I'm trying to fuck with your campaign, bruh. I'm not fuckin' with that nigga Bam. We need to link up."

"Link for what? What's up? Whe' is Bam?" was all Gangsta wanted to know. He wasn't trusting niggas these days.

"That's what I'm saying, bruh. I'm 'bout to meet up with Bam in a minute. I just want to formulate a plan so you can handle your business, and then we stick to the deal you presented," Monkey said.

"Y'all finna meet up?" skeptically Gangsta asked.

"Listen, bruh. Bam just murked ya boy Jay. Took his whole head off 'cause he got wind that you came over with that offer. Before this shit happened, though, he just dropped a hundred off. He made promises to double your offer once we found and killed you. The nigga fucked my partna Step right up, and he instantly started looking for you harder than the police was, bruh. And I wasn't with that. Plus Bam killing Jay wasn't cool. But Step showed he didn't give a fuck. That's why I took him out, and I'm keeping the hundred pounds, too."

"You took who out?" asked Gangsta.

"Step. I had to slump the nigga 'cause he want to follow Bam, and Bam a rat, bruh, plain and simple. I'd rather take my chances with you," Monkey said, but Gangsta didn't believe him for one second. He felt something was funny about it.

"How I know you not flexing me, though?"

"That's why I wanted to link up, so you can see, bruh. I will meet you anywhere, my nigga, standing in a pair of boxer shorts if I must. I'm just trying to move fast, 'cause I don't want Bam to get suspicious when me and Step 'posed to be out looking for you."

"Is that right?"

"On my kids."

"Ok, in two hours go back to that girl's house and wait on me there. I'm ready to die anyway, so if I see any sign of Bam or anything out of place, I'm killing you first, real talk," Gangsta stated and meant every word he said.

"Bet that," Monkey replied, then Gangsta hung up and called Nikki back to put her on point.

***

Ne-Ne

She was watching BET on the TV mounted to the wall when her room door cracked open slowly. She thought it had to be the nurse or doctor because visitation didn't begin for a couple more hours. It seemed a blur walked into her room. Ne-Ne instantly went into shock when she locked eyes with Gangsta. He closed the door as Ne-Ne sat up in her bed.

"Gary, what are you— Don't you know if somebody see you in here— What are you doing here?" Ne-Ne was confused.

"Nya, can you walk?" Gangsta ignored her questions, walking over to her bed. She was as beautiful as ever.

"Yes, why?"

"Come in the bathroom," Gangsta said and went into the tiny room.

Ne-Ne shook her head side-to-side. Gary was the last person she wanted to see at the moment, and it showed in her attitude. She swung her legs down to the floor, sliding her feet into her slippers. Using the railing of the bed, she got up and followed him into the bathroom. Gangsta looked drained when she walked in, and the stitches in his forehead made it look worse. She noticed his jeans were dirty and he reeked of a smell unlike himself. Ne-Ne pulled the door shut and leaned against the wall.

"What's up, Gary? What is it?" She was agitated.

"I need you, Nya. I'm sorry I failed y'all, and I'm doing everything in my power to make this right—"

"Make what right?" she cut him off, arms folded across her chest. "Your son is dying, Gary. Make what right?"

"Nya, I know! Damn you, acting like I'm the nigga who shot him or something like I was just out there in the streets starting shit. This fuck-shit came out of nowhere. I wasn't fucking with them niggas. I don't even know them suckas. Nya, I'm tore up inside, shawty. I'm weak as fuck, but I can't crumble 'cause I got a score to settle. I need you, though. I need you to believe in me and support—"

"I am supporting you. I can't wait for you to get the nigga behind this, but that still don't change the fact that our son is dying. And to be honest, it looks like we will have to bury him." Tears began to fall out of her eyes at the mention of their defeat. Gangsta's eyes began to water, also.

"Don't say that, Nya. Have you been praying?" He reached out to touch her, but she unfolded her arms and knocked his hand down.

"Yes, I pray! I'm just saying these doctors got me thinking that—"

"Nya!" Gangsta crowded her space, tears now falling fast down his face as well as hers. He took her shoulders in both hands, bending down to eyelevel with her.

"Fuck what they saying. Anyways, I thought he was being sent to Grady for the surgery," Gangsta said.

"Surgery is in two days, and he left last night. I will be going home tomorrow, so I'm going straight there when I'm released."

"Ok, cool. Well, here. Call me from this number and keep me updated." He pulled out a phone, gave it to her, then kissed her forehead.

"Mrs. Robertson?"

At the sound of her name, they both jumped. Ne-Ne placed her finger to her lips, telling him to be quite as she walked out, closing the bathroom door back and glad to see it was the young nurse she was cool with.

"Yes?"

"Doctor Greene said you can leave today if you choose to because you're ready. I told her yes 'cause I figured you wanted to see your son and all, so she's getting your discharge papers right now," the young, pretty nurse said. She and Ne-Ne became cool over the few days spent together.

"Ok, that's fine. Listen, have you seen any one of them detectives walking around or anything?" Ne-Ne asked.

"No, I haven't. But if I do, do you want me to send them up?" the nurse replied with her own question.

"No, I just wanted to know, that's all. Thank you, though, for everything." Ne-Ne and the nurse hugged, then she left the room. Ne-Ne quickly walked back into the bathroom to find Gangsta sitting on the edge of the toilet.

"I'm about to leave. You gotta go," she spoke, standing in the door of the bathroom. Gangsta stood and walked up on her.

"Ne-Ne, do you believe in me?" He towered over her small frame.

Ne-Ne looked up in his eyes. She witnessed so much pain. She saw defeat in him more than she had ever seen. His eyes were cold and black, his soul was burning, and this she knew. Ne-Ne looked away and thought about her reply. She looked back up into his eyes and spoke.

"To be honest, I don't, but I truly hope you surprise me."

Gangsta just stared at her for a minute, then he nodded his head up and down before stepping around her, leaving the room. Ne-Ne knew her statement would crush him, but it was exactly how she felt: crushed, hurtful, and hateful. She shed one more tear, but this one was for the end of them. Her heart told her it was truly over. His facial expression just showed her more coldness about their situation, and even toward her. It was a look she had never seen on Gangsta, one that made her wish she would've lied and hidden her feelings instead of bringing it to him for real. There was no denying the fact that she did love Gary, and she did believe in him. Though she was also scared and felt unsafe, she was rooting for him to succeed and not fail.

To her, Gangsta was one of the realist guys she knew. He had grace about himself, and at all times he was calm and humble, but there was no over-painting — he was most definitely from the hood. Overall, Gangsta was solid. He always kept it real and was one of those guys who always was willing to help people in any form or fashion. It was a trait she liked about him, and everyone around him felt the same.

Chapter 10

Bam

Trina was cuddled up under him, asleep. Bam reached for his phone to see if he had any missed calls. His messages showed a picture text from his babymama and a few text messages from miscellaneous people, but none from Monkey or step saying they received the package. He climbed out of the bed, looking back at his rider. He deciding to leave her asleep. He got dressed and rolled a blunt in the living room. He called his bodyguard, who was already downstairs waiting on him when he got to the lobby. He was met by his main bodyguard.

"Boss, what's up? You good?" the bodyguard asked, leading the way out of the lobby. Bam only nodded his reply as he followed. He pulled his phone out and opened the picture message from his babymama. He knew it was a picture of his kids, like she always sent, or one of them long-ass messages telling him how much she loved him and missed him. Goldie always knew the correct words to say to him, and at the correct moments. He climbed into the back of the awaiting Benz as the message downloaded.

"Where to, boss?" The driver looked at him through the mirror.

Bam looked up and said, "Take me to Monkey and Step's spot. These niggas acting like they can't contact me on my business, yo. I'm just not with that."

The picture message failed to download. Bam realized he didn't have a strong signal, so he called Goldie instead, only to get her voicemail. He tired once more to get the same thing, so he dialed her mother's house and the phone just rang, so he hung up.

When Bam made it to the trap house of Monkey and Step, only a few shooters stood on the porch. Bam was introduced to a dude named Mack, who ran the spot. Inside the trap house, people sat around with long faces and saddened mugs.

"Son, where is Monkey and Step," Bam asked once inside the house. Mack cleared his throat.

"Police just found this nigga, Step, dead over there off Bankhead, him and another nigga slumped in somebody's driveway," Mack said.

"Another dude?" Bam faced Mack. "Where is Monkey?"

"Yeah, another dude. Matter fact, Monkey and Pam just left about an hour ago. He took all the product with them only leaving me ten pounds to get off. Fucked up thing is after Monkey left, Step's uncle and mom pulled up hysterical, looking for Monkey. She said that she just left the morgue, that the police found Step dead. Shot in the face," Mack explained while he followed Bam as he continued to walk throughout the trap house, processing all he was hearing. Now it all made sense why he wasn't receiving calls from Step or Monkey.

"Yo, son, text the nigga Monkey and tell him that you done with them ten, that you need some more." Bam gave orders like the boss he was. His two bodyguards stood inside the house as well, waiting on the word from Bam to clear the house out. Mack did as told.

Bam took his own phone out and again downloaded the message from Goldie that failed earlier. When the message opened up and Bam saw the picture, his heart stopped. He raised the phone to his face, opened his eyes wider to get a better look, making sure he saw what he thought he saw and who it was. Bam's hands instantly started trembling as he stared at his babymama with a bullet hole in her cheekbone, eyes wide open, blank with no life in them. He didn't understand at first. He didn't even wanna believe this happened. It had to be a joke. But this was the wrong time to be joking, and Goldie knew this, but Goldie didn't play games. She was too woman for that. Bam looked at the picture again and dialed her number, and again he got the voicemail. Bam then quickly strolled down the contact list and made a call to one of his people to pull up around on South Miami Avenue, but Bam got the news he didn't want to hear.

It was all over the news that five people were killed, which included his babymama, but his kids were safe in police custody. That was the best news of all, that his kids didn't get hurt.

"What the fuck," Bam said to his own self while hanging up the phone. His stomach was in knots as Gangsta crossed his mind.

Mack's phone had started to ring. Bam walked over and said, "Put it on speaker."

"What's up, bruh?" Mack answered and put it on speakerphone, as requested.

"What's up? You text and said that network gone already?"

It was Monkey. Bam nodded his head, then indicated a money signal with his hand.

"Yeah, I got all the paper," Mack said into the phone, catching on to what Bam was saying.

"Damn, shit booming today, huh? I'ma drop you off ten more in a few hours. I got some shit I need you to do," Monkey shot back.

Bam, on the other hand, shook his head at Mack, then walked over and whispered in his ear.

"Tell 'im you need the shit now. You got niggas' money already. Tell him you will meet him somewhere."

"Bruh, I got extra paper on top of what I owe you. Niggas gave me money up front. I need dis shit, like, yesterday. I can meet you, though, if that's the case," Mack did as told.

Monkey was silent for a moment before he replied. "Ok, Pam will bring it to you in the next thirty minutes. Just be on point and give her the bread. I got to go, bruh. I will check in later."

"Bet that," Mack confirmed once Bam agreed with a shake of his head. They hung up the phone, then Bam walked up on Mack.

"Yo, son, who is this Pam chick?"

***

Monkey

"Baby girl, I need you to take Mack ten mo' pounds. Get that money, too, from him while I go handle this business with Gangsta," Monkey told Pam as they sat in the hotel room with ninety pounds.

"So you don't need me shotgun with you meeting the dude?" she asked, picking up her strap from the table.

"Naw, I'm just 'bout to do this quick as possible so I can call Bam. I know the nigga worried, and I don't want him to start thinking something is up. I want it to be a surprise when Gangsta pop up and murk his ass." Monkey could wait for it. Step's mother was already blowing his phone up. He refused to answer. He hated the fact she found out so fast, but at the same time, he knew with him killing Step in someone's driveway in the open, someone would report it sooner rather than later.

"Ok, and we meet back here, right?" Pam questioned.

"Yeah," replied Monkey.

Pam agreed to meet with Mack while he handled his business. Monkey hit the streets after he got strapped up, ready to get this shit over with. He headed back to Nikki's house with hopes that Gangsta would now believe he wasn't with Bam. Even though he didn't know Gangsta, Monkey felt something real about him. Monkey hardly trusted people, but he'd rather take his chances with Gangsta than fuckin' with a snitch.

Leaving the hotel, Monkey smoothly walked to the rental SUV, wishing it had tints on all the windows instead of just the back. He knew he had to be extra careful with his movement going over to Gangsta and hoped like hell that everything worked like a clock, because if not, then everything would be exposed and it would be a for sure war. Monkey was a hustler, not a killer. But if need be, he wouldn't hesitate to take one out. Though it wasn't his thing, he liked to grind. All Monkey wanted was the money and a way out of the game, because at the end of the road there was only jail and death, and he was ready for neither.

He made it to the west side of Atlanta and instantly became nervous as he exited the highway, turning onto Bankhead. He made two right turns, passing the Blue Flame and Tower Liquor Store. As soon as he passed, he heard his phone ring. It was a private number, meaning it was Gangsta.

"Hello," Monkey answered.

"Turn around and pull into the Tower Liquor Store," Gangsta's voice said. Monkey's eyes started scanning everywhere as he drove, looking for a place to turn around. He felt like Gangsta was right behind him in the backseat, hovering over him. *Where is this nigga, Monkey?*

All of a sudden his nervousness turned into fear. He rode back up the street at a snail's pace, watching both sides of the street. Something wasn't right, his gut was telling him. And at that thought, Monkey decided to hightail it out of there. But it was as if Gangsta heard his thoughts.

"Pull into the club to your right," Gangsta spoke, and without thought Monkey whipped into the club parking lot. His heart now in his stomach, experiencing the worst needle-and-pins in each of his fingers as he crept through, the tires crunching the gravel as he inched forward. Monkey stopped breathing when he heard Gangsta.

"Get out. Get in the car to your left," Gangsta said, and that's when Monkey turned to see him sitting in the backseat of a car. Gangsta held a gun aimed at Monkey's face with the beam on bright. Careful not to panic, Monkey complied and parked the SUV. He got out with his own gun on him, but concealed. Monkey walked over to the other door, but Gangsta pointed to the driver's seat. Monkey got the idea and climbed into the car, closing the door, both hands partially in the air.

"I'm not against you, my nigga, real talk. You can put down the gun." Monkey wanted to calm him down before he even got started.

"Pull off, my nigga," was the only thing Gangsta said, then pressed the cold steal to the back of Monkey's head, who in return cranked up and mashed the gas. He turned the car around. Monkey pulled out, going to the left.

"Did anybody follow you?" Gangsta lowered the gun.

"Naw, my nigga, everything good, bruh," replied Monkey, then added, "I'm tryna lay this nigga Bam at your feet. I'm not the enemy, bruh. I know you can't trust niggas, but I'm not the one that wants you hurt, bruh."

"Pull up in the first parking lot to your right," Gangsta demanded when they rode down to Dogwood Apartments, and Monkey followed instructions. He pulled into the parking lot.

"You got a gun on your person?" was Gangsta's next question, because he could not afford to slip right now.

"Yeah, I'm strapped." Monkey was being honest.

"If you expect me to trust you, then I got to have that gun. It ain't nothing personal, pimp. I'm just not giving nobody the up. I don't care who you are," Gangsta said as Monkey parked the car. He didn't even respond as he grabbed the gun from his waist and handed it over to Gangsta. He was ready to get Bam out of the way. He was the biggest threat of them all. Gangsta got out of the car and Monkey did the same.

"Let's ride." Gangsta climbed into an all-black Cutlass 442 with heavy tints. Monkey jumped into the driver's seat. Gangsta passed him the keys.

Chapter 11

Bam

Bam had to stay focused, even though his babymama being dead was heavy on his mind. He wanted revenge so bad on anybody he could get his hands on. He wanted to know who was truly behind the murders, because he would make them pay dearly. He couldn't figure out if Gangsta was the one who did this, how did he get the location on Goldie? He underestimated Gangsta and his help. He wouldn't do it a second time, he promised.

Bam, Mack, and the bodyguards were the only ones in the trap house, waiting on Pam to pull up. He made everyone else leave because it may get bloody with how he was feeling. Bam wasn't an emotional type of person, but he was bothered about his babymama and how easy it was to find him or his family. He paced the living room floor, looking at his phone, waiting on the call about his kids being picked up by family. Plus he expected a call from Monkey at any time with the slick shit, but little did Monkey know, Bam had done figured his bullshit out. As soon as Bam could get his hands on Monkey, he would die in a painful way. Bam vowed in his heart to do Monkey something bad. For some strange reason, he started wishing he'd never been introduced to Gangsta, that it was the wrong move to ever fuck with him, and even more messed up that he went at the man, because now it has turned into a war instead of Bam coming out on top like he had planned when he made the choice to ransom this stupid nigga.

It didn't take Pam thirty minutes to pull into the yard. Bam watched from the window as she got out of the whip, throwing a book bag over her shoulders. She was a fine lil' something, Bam noticed, but fuck what she looking like, because pussy was the last thing on his mind.

Mack opened the door for Pam. Just as soon as she stepped through the door, both bodyguards attacked her. Pam was caught off guard when the two massive dudes snatched her up, then Bam pulled out his gun. He pushed it into her face and twisted it into her smooth skin.

"You got only one chance to tell me where I can find Monkey, where is my product, and what the fuck is Monkey's plan. And bitch, you better not lie," Bam said through gritted teeth. Both of her arms were held. Bam took the opportunity to relieve her of the gun on her hip.

"What's up, Mack?" was the question she asked, looking up to her so-called friend. Bam tucked her gun, then slapped the taste out of her mouth. He started choking her, then got close to her ear.

"Bitch, you must didn't hear me?"

"Okay." She was losing her breath. Bam let her neck go. "First of all, I don't have shit to do with y'all business. Ask Monkey."

"Bitch!" Bam went back at her neck.

"Please," Pam screamed and tried desperately to hide her throat. This was the last thing she expected to happen. Now Monkey and Step had gotten her caught up in some bullshit. "Listen, Monkey just asked me to help ride with him, that's it."

"Wrong answer." Bam cocked his gun back and aimed at her face.

"Just tell him what's up, Pam. Don't go out like this," Mack warned her. He didn't want to see her die by the hands of this maniac when she really didn't have nothing to do with what was going on. Overall, Pam was good people. She was loyal and had an eye for the hustle. She just was the hood freak, but the hood had grown to love her. Sweat beads started to form and slide down her face. She looked from Mack to Bam and back to Mack.

"Ok. Ok, alright. Monkey is going to meet Gangsta right now. They gonna try and corner you. That's all I know, I swear," Pam pleaded with great fear. She wasn't ready to die, but Bam wasn't going for it.

"Bitch, tell me everything. I mean every single detail." He pressed the gun into her skin some more.

"All I know is that Monkey said he killed Step 'cause Step was trying to help you, and he wanted me to help him move the weed from this spot to another trap house. Monkey wouldn't tell me everything, but I do know he's going to meet Gangsta at some apartments on Bankhead."

"Do you know where it's located?" Bam asked.

"Yeah, exactly," Pam replied, hoping this would get her a pass. Bam lowered the gun and backed off her. He nodded to his bodyguards to release her. She fell to the ground. Bam turned around on Mack, raised the pistol to his face, and pulled the trigga.

Boom!

Mack's body hit the ground. Bam stood over him and shot two more times.

Boom! Boom!

"Yo, let's ride," he spoke and walked off, leaving Mack slumped in the trap house.

Not even ten minutes later, Bam got a call from Monkey.

"Yo, son, where you niggas at? I thought y'all ran off with that lil' shit." Bam tried to sound normal even though he was boiling on the inside. He couldn't wait to get his hands on Monkey and to get this shit over with Gangsta.

"Yeah, we got half of it knocked out already. Fuck all that, though. I know where this nigga Gangsta is hiding out. Me and Step been watching him all day."

"Oh, word?"

"Hell yeah. So what's up? How do you want to play this shit?" Monkey asked.

"I'm pulling up to where you at right now, son. Is y'all still posted where this nigga at?"

"Yeah, I'm about to text you the address," Monkey replied, then they hung up. Bam made a call to order up a team of gunners. He rode shotgun with Pam next to him. He held the pistol down between his legs, waiting on her to try anything.

The text came through. It was an address on Hollywood Road. When Bam saw it, he just laughed and gave his driver directions to get there. *So he wants war, huh?* Bam thought and laughed again. Gangsta wasn't ready to take it there. He called Trina.

"Daddy," she instantly picked up.

"Yo, ma. I need you to call your wild-ass cousins. Tell them I need me a couple of shooters, and check on your dresser. I left you some instructions to handle for me," Bam said to his rider.

"Ok, Daddy. I got it, but is everything alright?" Trina had never seen him call for niggas who weren't part of his team, so it was strange that he told her to get her people involved. She knew Bam and knew that some major stuff was going down, and she wanted to be there for her nigga as she always was.

"Yeah, shorty, everything lovely," Bam lied, and she instantly peeped it, but said nothing about it.

The first place Bam stopped was on Simpson when he made it to the west side. He had a team of gunners from the bluff who were somewhat linked up with Lucky. Bam was certified to use them at his will when he needed the help. The driver pulled his Benz up into a dirty yard with too many cars packed on the property. Bam was out of the Benz as soon as it stopped. There were at least twelve niggas in the yard, none loyal to Bam, but one guy named Killer was a Blood member, and every other dude in the yard was a Blood who was loyal to Killer. Bam dapped him up as they bumped shoulders.

"So, tell me what's going on, dog?" Killer asked.

"Yo, son, a nigga just clapped my babymama and her whole family down in Miami. I got beef with this fuck-nigga over here on

Hollywood Road who is behind this Miami hit. I underestimated him once already, so I'm not trying to play with this nigga again, son," Bam explained, then went on to tell Killer about Monkey and what he was trying to do. He explained the situation with Pam and all. He needed the help, and he did not have time to fuck around. Killer listened, then agreed to link up with Bam because he owed him an act of loyalty.

"Dog, you know that I'm going out on a limb for you by lending my shooters. I can get dub for this shit, my nigga, so make sure my young niggas come back safe."

"Yo' word is bond. They will be safe, and I will break each one of them lil' niggas off a nice check for their trouble," Bam assured Killer.

If something went wrong, then it was Killer's ass on the line for putting Bloods in the business. When Bam pulled off, he pulled off with eight Blood members, all strapped with plans to kill.

Chapter 12

Gangsta

All he could do was think about how he was gonna do Bam once he caught him. Gangsta could taste his blood, couldn't wait to see the look in his eyes. All Bam had to do was pull up, and it's a wrap.

Gangsta still wasn't trusting Monkey. He was watching every move Monkey was making, but Gangsta got put at ease when Monkey made the call to set Bam up. It showed that he was real. Monkey was looking out the window, ready for Bam so he could see the look on his face, eager to see the outcome, to get this day over with so he could get to the money.

Gangsta also had a few niggas around with him, ready to prove their loyalty to him, and people who knew Gangsta knew he was a real nigga with a good heart. Gangsta had Nikki and Roxanne in hiding with their kids. Nikki's baby daddy Poonie and his two partnas rode along with Gangsta, because none of them from Hollywood Road fucked with Bam. Zay and Eric were the only two niggas who rocked with that nigga.

Everyone in the living room had choppers with extended clips, and everyone was ready to die or kill something, especially Gangsta.

"We got action," Monkey said from the window, seeing a car rolling down the block. Gangsta got to the window and looked out.

"Step on the porch. Show your face," Gangsta spoke, looking at the all-black Tahoe truck. It stopped in front of the address given.

"Bruh, I'm not stepping—"

The ringing of his cell phone scared the life out of Monkey. He nearly jumped out of his skin. He picked up, knowing the caller was Bam.

"'Lo?"

"I'm out here, son. Where you at?" Bam asked.

The entire block was deserted, not a soul in sight. Gangsta had two niggas across the street on standby just in case things got out of hand. he had a guy ready at three of the houses on the block, hidden from the scene, ready to surprise Bam. This was the moment Gangsta had been waiting on. Today Bam would not make it out alive. Gangsta was doing this for the old and the new — especially the new.

Before Gangsta knew it, he hung the chopper out the window and let off two bursts. The bullets struck the truck, and the squad followed his lead, also busting their guns as the Tahoe tried to pull off from the scene. Poonie and his best friend, Twan, ran out the door to give chase to the shot-up SUV. The driver had to be dead, because the truck rolled into the curb and stopped. Gangsta was about to run out behind Poonie until he looked out the window and saw niggas creeping on foot. He raised the chopper, aimed at one of the many dudes, and shot, picking him off and making Poonie duck. Men on Gangsta's side came from around the houses, spread out, devouring Bam's men who were on foot.

War started on the street. Poonie took cover and started busting his shots at four or five more niggas, all holding guns with two hands. Monkey joined in from the window, and Poonie's other partna, Nard, was keeping the niggas from overpowering Poonie. Two more trucks turned on the block.

That's when Gangsta stepped out, determined to kill every nigga who was against him. Monkey and the rest followed Gangsta's lead. They wouldn't allow the niggas in the trucks to get into position. Everything looked like Swiss cheese. The trucks were surrounded by bodies, sprawled out dead in the streets. Gangsta ran up on the first truck. He snatched open the door to take a look inside and found no Bam.

"Fuck," he stated and quickly checked the other two whip. There was no Bam in sight.

Gangsta was pissed, but kinda knew that Bam was a bit smarter than to be trapped. He looked up the block just in time to see a Benz creeping by with its back window let down. He and Bam stared at each other. Gangsta was about to aim his chopper, but the Benz pulled off.

Poonie and Gangsta were the first to take off running in the opposite direction. The other people followed as they all cut through the woods, running downhill. Gangsta wasn't expecting it to go like this, but he couldn't just sit back and be attacked like some fuck-nigga. He lost it because he wanted Bam dead so bad that he forgot the plan.

Poonie jumped over two fences as the police sirens were blaring louder and louder. Gangsta didn't miss a beat, jumping the same two gates, keeping up with Poonie. They all ran at least a mile through the woods, coming out at the bottom of Hollywood Road.

Everyone split up, but Gangsta and Monkey walked together out of the woods and into some more across the street. As soon as they were fully in the woods, both guys took off running again. This was Gangsta's neck of the wood, so he led the way to Mango Circle and ran down the street to Bolton Road. It took them another fifteen minutes to walk to Bankhead where Monkey's ride was parked. They both jumped in, out of breath but glad to be off Hollywood Road and safe in a car. Moments later, Monkey cranked up, pulled off, and quickly hit the highway.

***

Ne-Ne

Ne-Ne, crying, stood when she saw the doctor exit her office. Erica and Terry were also with her, standing behind her as her support. Junior was still in surgery and Ne-Ne desperately wanted to know what was going on with her baby, but nobody said anything, so she decided to talk to the head doctor herself.

"Excuse me, ma'am. I'm Ms. Rober—"

"I know who you are. Surgery is a long process, depending. So I'm not answering any questions pertaining, yes?"

The doctor was direct, but Ne-Ne didn't accept it. She looked the woman straight in the eyes.

"Is there any sign of a chance?" Ne-Ne's heart was hurting, tears falling from her face. She wouldn't stop crying. She couldn't stop crying. She needed hope. She wanted God to answer her prayers and heal her son. Ne-Ne was ready to give her own life for her son.

The doctor looked down to the floor. She snickered, then looked back up to Ne-Ne.

"I guess you think I'm not stressed, too, just 'cause it's your son in there, huh? Well, if you don't already know, it's his life in my hands if the surgery doesn't go right. I'm not trying to be mean or an ass, but let me do my job, ma'am, and you continue to pray." The doctor walked around Ne-Ne, who was about to reply until Mrs. Jackson stepped out of the doctor's office. Ne-Ne ran over to her.

"Mrs. Jackson, what's going on?" Ne-Ne asked since Gangsta's mom was the head nurse at Grady now.

"Baby, I can't say. Just say nothing bad has happened, but something happened. We just don't know what it was, so they are running tests before surgery continues. Just cross your fingers and thank God, because he is already working." Mrs. Jackson hugged Ne-Ne.

"Thank you, thank you, thank you. Thank you so much, Mrs. Jackson," Ne-Ne said. Erica joined in on the embrace, then Terry.

"Now, y'all go get some food in y'all and come on back here while Doctor Carmela fixes our Junior," Mrs. Jackson told the girls, who all agreed because nobody had really eaten anything since all this started. Everyone instantly became happy and hopeful. Ne-Ne finally smiled at the good news they heard. She just wished the doctor would've been helpful like Mrs. Jackson was, but Ne-Ne wasn't on that anymore.

"Thank you again, Mrs. Jackson. I love you." Ne-Ne spoke from the heart.

The girls left Grady with two Mexican escorts. They rode in an all-black range rover with heavy tints. There was a lot of activity in front of the hospital when they were leaving. Ne-Ne caught a glimpse of people being rushed into the hospital laid out on stretchers. There were a couple ambulances, and everyone was moving fast. Ne-Ne wondered what that was about and fearfully pondered who they were.

"Where to, ma'am?" one of the Mexicans asked as the truck was en route. Erica, who was big on places to eat, sat up right in her seat.

"Applebee's or Red Lobster. Which one, sis?" She turned to Ne-Ne.

"Red Lobster." Ne-Ne replied, because she liked the atmosphere and vibe at Red Lobster, and they took their time and cooked the food correctly. Plus being at a sit-down restaurant gave her a break from the stress of being in the hospital. It was some time to think good thoughts.

Ne-Ne turned to the Mexican in the passenger's seat. "Turn it to the news station, please." As soon as he complied, the reporter announced there had been a huge shootout on Hollywood Road that left six dead and four injured. They had one suspect in custody.

"Damn, I hope that ain't none of my people," Terry said out of nowhere, and Erica agreed with a nod of her head.

Ne-Ne pulled out the phone Gangsta gave her. She found the contact and pressed send. Her heart raced in her chest as the phone began to ring. She was praying Gangsta was ok. She didn't want him hurt. She was tired of people she loved being hurt. It just needed to all stop and go back to normal like the life she knew. The price paid for loving a street nigga is not what she expected, and if she would've known things like this would happen, Gangsta would have had a choice.

"Whoa," he picked up.

"Are you ok?" She was happy to hear his voice.

"Yeah, in the trenches," replied Gangsta. "What's up with Junior? How did surgery go?" he asked, concerned.

"It's still going. So you sure you ok, right?" Ne-Ne decided not to give him the news about their son just yet.

"As ok as I'ma be. You know what's on my mind. Look though, I got to go, baby girl. I will check with you in a few hours," Gangsta said, then they both hung up and Ne-Ne truly felt better. It was like weights being lifted up off of her.

***

Gangsta

After Gangsta and Monkey split up, he was picked up by Jeter at the train station. He was glad to have made it out alive without a scratch, but hated the fact Bam slipped through the cracks of death. Gangsta remembered seeing the Benz Bam rode in. He saw his face clear as day, a face he wouldn't forget. As the truck cruised up I-85, Gangsta turned on Bam's babymama's cellphone to get Bam's number out of the contacts. He cleaned the phone of all possible prints, then tossed it out the window. It shattered in his rearview.

Bam would pay dearly for all he had done in Atlanta. Nothing and nobody will stop this murder.

Jeter lit up a blunt and passed it. Gangsta's mind was in limbo on many different things, but mainly his son invaded his thoughts. His plan was almost coming together. He was sure hoping it worked, and only God could see that it would. He hit the blunt two hard times, then inhaled and held it until he couldn't anymore.

The streets had gotten bloody tonight, and this was only the beginning of the war. The only issue he had was the men Bam had. He needed a team to go at this nigga, because it showed today that Bam wasn't playing fair, so Gangsta had to tighten up. He knew the opportunity would present itself for an easy kill, he just wished it was sooner rather than later. Gangsta knew the Feds were on Bam and he had to be extra careful, because they were at Bam's house and almost every place he went. They somehow were following him, except for the times when he straight-up lost them. But when the Feds were not around, his bodyguards were, and a small army of stupid niggas. It was going to be hard to get at Bam unless he made Bam come out, but that, too, would be hard because of today's actions.

When they finally made it to Gwinnett County, Gangsta was told to shower and get dressed for the dinner meeting with Loco's father and grandfather. Loco had fresh cloths and shoes laid out for him. Gangsta found the bathroom and stripped down.

The water felt good to his body. He relaxed under the warm stream of water as his thoughts reverted back to Junior and his wellbeing. Gangsta said a quick prayer, then began to bathe his sore body. He was mentally exhausted, physically drained, and heartbroken, more helpless than he'd ever been. He regretted everything he'd ever done to get to this point. If he had known his son would be the sacrifice, he would never have tried the game or anything pertaining to it. All he wanted was for his team to be on top, like a lot of niggas he knew. He wanted his family straight and their pockets full. He didn't expect his own brother to snitch him out. He never saw Kash catching a life sentence coming into the picture. It took one nigga to bring them down, and it seemed a miracle to bring them out of the hole Dank dug for them. So much bullshit had happened since he got out of prison. Niggas had changed, and the game was sour.

After he got dressed, Loco met him at the bottom of the steps. They walked out of the house to the waiting Benz truck. The night air felt good on Gangsta's skin.

"You feel better, I hope, my friend?" Loco asked when they both sat comfortably in the leather seats.

"Hell yeah, I feel pretty good, way. That shower did it."

"Good to know, my friend," replied Loco, and the remainder of the ride was in silence. Loco looked ahead as Gangsta texted Ne-Ne back and forth. She told him a little girl got shot by a stray bullet on Hollywood Road. She was in critical condition, and the police had one guy in custody already. Gangsta wondered who it was that got caught, but he didn't ask her. Instead, he asked for his family back. He asked for her love, her forgiveness, and her support — but he never received an answer back.

Minutes later the Benz pulled up to a very large home with so many cars lining the circle driveway. The house was so big that it looked like a shopping center from the streets. Loco and Gangsta were escorted inside the large place and greeted by the doorman. Soft music was playing on the overhead speakers throughout the house. They were led into a den area where Jeter, Longo, and Melody all sat at a bar. Mya was seated next to a very old man, short and skinny with white hair. The house was crowded, but mostly with help, such as security, maids, cooks, and then family. Loco introduced Gangsta to a man standing over by the picture frame window.

"Father, I would like you to meet my dear friend, Gangsta, the young man I've been speaking about lately. Gangsta, this is my father, Chavez, and my Papa, Mr. Play."

Gangsta nodded his respect. Chavez turned and sized him up. He locked eyes with Gangsta before speaking.

"How you, son?" Chavez's English was clear. Unlike the rest of them in the house, he was a broad man with just as much height as Gangsta. His hair wasn't gray — it was black, long, and curly. He wore rings on nearly all of his fingers and a long chain around his neck. Chavez looked like money, looked just like he was a drug dealer. He stuck his hand out and Gangsta embraced it.

"I'm doing ok, Mr. Chavez."

"Well, I've heard all good things about you, so before leaving I wanted to meet the man himself that got nearly all my security at his beck and call. Loco pulled an ace card for you, my friend, which mean there's something he sees in you," Chavez spoke, then led Gangsta over to the old man and Mya.

"Father." Chavez introduced Gangsta to the old man. He only waved his hand. He couldn't speak English, but his smile was welcoming, his eyes were bright, and Gangsta could tell he was the man.

"You missed dinner already, but we can get you a plate," Mya added.

"I'm good."

"Well, come join me for a drink," Chavez cut in, seeing his daughter's eyes full of Gangsta, who wasn't paying any of her gestures attention. And that was something Chavez liked.

They walked into a kitchen that was the size of a store, and Chavez made everyone leave so they could talk privately. He fixed up two stiff shots and took a seat on the countertop. Gangsta did the same. They both downed their drinks, making their faces ball up from the strong taste.

"So, tell me why is it you and Bam are at war, my friend?" Chavez asked.

Gangsta looked down into his empty cup, shaking his head before he said, "That nigga wanted me to work for him and I wouldn't." Gangsta explained the entire thing from the first day they met up until the kidnapping. He also made sure to thank Chavez for lending his help.

"I pray for you and your family. You seem like a good kid, very smart like Loco said and humble like never before. You don't meet them like you anymore, so I embrace the decision Loco has made to make you a part of our team. See, my friend, in war it's not always about who can kill the most people or who has the biggest gun. It's about the support you have behind your actions. It takes money and loyalty most of all to win a war. Now I can send you 1000 men and you can go kill your entire hood, or I can give you 1000 kilos and you can build your team strong to take down whoever, wherever, whenever. I hate that this has happened to your son, and I know your heart is in it. But see, I know Bam, and he's going into hiding because the stove is too hot for him. But he is smart and clever, so you need to get like him and sit back, build your team, and then declare war."

Chavez had poured them up another shot. Gangsta was feeling what Chavez was saying, but at the same time he didn't have time to waste. He could not let this nigga get away. He would find and murder Bam. It was a known saying: *You can run, but you can't hide.* Gangsta vowed to hunt him down like the dog he was and do him the nasty way.

Chavez passed Gangsta the drink and turned his own up. He wiped his mouth with the back of his hand.

"I feel that, but I got to get this dude before he get away. I'm grateful you would even trust me with that much product, but I gotta take a rain check."

Gangsta downed his drink. Chavez fixed another one.

"I knew you would say that. See, you got heart and balls, but right now you are speaking through emotions, not common sense. Maybe soon you will understand, but you have made your choice. And as a father, I will ride with you. Understand I can no longer involve my people to assist you anymore, but security for your family will stay the same. My business must continue, and when all this is over with, my offer is still on the table."

"I understand that, and thank you again, Mr. Chavez. I sure wish the circumstances were different." Gangsta was feeling the effects of the liquor. He didn't want to turn the connection down like he did, but he didn't want to commit to a deal yet on consignment, because right now anything could happen.

"No, I understand you, amigo. Trust me. But thinking before acting is the best key. I will tell my son, when you are ready, to give you the product." Chavez downed one more drink before they went back into the den.

Jerry Jackson

Chapter 13

Kash

"Charles McCants." The officer called his name from the other side of the door. Kash was lying back on his bunk, reading a novel. He turned his head toward the cell door and voice. He saw more than one officer's shadow from the bottom of the door. Kash sat up. "Yeah." Kash stood, sliding his feet into a pair of shower shoes. He walked to the cell door as the window flap was being opened. He saw Sergeant Keller and two COs. The Sergeant held a pair of handcuffs. "What's up, Sergeant?"

"Attorney visit," one of the COs said, and one of the officers opened the tray flap. Kash stuck both hands out from behind to be cuffed.

High max was nothing like he expected it to be. It was much better than the many different stories he'd heard over the years. It was laid back, and Kash knew half the niggas in his unit who were already plugged in with various ways to make movement happen. Kash wondered what this lawyer visit was about and hoped it wasn't anything bad. He didn't need bad news right now. It was bad enough he had a life sentence — a fresh life that was starting to aggravate him. The Sergeant led him to the warden's office, where his high-priced lawyer sat behind the desk in his expensive suit. He opened a folder, then cleared his throat.

"First, how are you?" he questioned, and continued, "Your parents retained me. Apparently they want you to give your guilty plea back." The lawyer was reading from the paperwork.

Now Kash was even more dumbfounded. What were his parents doing, he wondered.

"Take my plea back?" responded Kash, confused.

"Yes. I need your signature on both sheets so I can get the ball rolling. I will have you in court in no less than thirty days." The lawyer pushed the papers across to Kash. He got them and read them carefully, then signed and gave the papers back.

"So what's the grounds? What's the plan once we get back in court?" Kash wanted to know what was going on.

"I will know in a few days. I'm also meeting with your warden today so we can get you proper phone calls. Here is my number, also. You can call anytime. I'll accept."

He and the lawyer shook hands as they stood. Kash was led back to his cell and locked in. Now his mind was in overdrive, because something was going on and he was lost. He'd been in high max two weeks now and still hadn't heard from anyone of importance. He was hoping the Feds did not snatch up Gangsta in the sweep they did in Atlanta. Kash had only received one letter, and it came from his babymama, Ebony, telling him to write his kids and leaving her number for him to call collect.

Kash walked to his cell door. He got on the floor and looked out into the unit. The crack under the door was small enough to see through, but not big like the tray flap was. Only one orderly was out cleaning.

"Say, orderly! Come to room 206," Kash yelled through the crack at the bottom of the cell door he saw the orderly throw up one hand, indicating he understood. Meco was also on high max, plugged in already. Kash needed to use his phone, because now he was worried and wanted to know what was up with this lawyer shit all of a sudden. Moments later, the orderly opened Kash's flap. Kash gave him a small note to take to Meco.

"Come right back. Let me know what he say," he reminded the orderly.

"Got you," he said and walked away. Kash sat back on his bunk and picked up the letter from Ebony. She was concerned and he knew it. A couple of minutes later the orderly returned with a note and a cell phone.

Whoa, what's mobbin', bruh? I miss you, nigga! Go ahead and use the hook. You got an hour, foo'. The orderly will come pick it up at the time. Come outside when they call yard. Do you got food?

Kash read and flushed the note. He took a seat on the bunk. The first person he called was his mother. She picked up on the third ring.

"Hello?"

"This Charles, ma."

"Charles! Oh my God, how are you, baby?" Her soft, humble voice became excited from hearing her son. It made Kash smile.

"I'm holding up, ma. This lawyer came today. You wanna tell me what's going on?" he asked.

"Yes. Ebony called and said your friend Gary requested that you give back your plea. He said he has a plan. Me and your dad had a talk and decided that it was a good idea. What's the worst that could happen?"

She had a point, he couldn't lie. "Do you got a number on Gary?" He needed to get in touch with his brother.

"No, I don't, but call Ebony. Baby, Gary is in a lot of trouble. A lot has happened since you been in, son."

"Ok, ma. I love you. Tell dad the same. I will write you. I'm about to call Ebony."

He and his mom disconnected, leaving him more confused than ever. *Gangsta was in big trouble.* He wondered what was this big trouble his brother was in. All these questions Kash needed answered.

When Ebony picked up the phone, she was at work at her desk. "Detective Wright speaking."

"Ebony, what's up? Can you talk?"

"Charles! Oh my gosh, how are you? Did you get my— Well, I know you got the letter. How are you—"

"What's up with Gangsta?" Kash cut her off with a question. He was worried, and she heard it in his voice, so she didn't keep him waiting.

"Ok, so his babymama and son was kidnapped. The son got shot in the head. Apparently cops say Gary killed the kidnappers and now he's wanted, long story short."

"His son got shot?" was his next question.

"Yes, he's on life support. The mother was shot, too. It's been a lot of murders in Atlanta since then, and on Hollywood Road six people were killed and more was hurt. A little girl got shot by a stray bullet. The Feds have picked that case up, and Gangsta was wanted for triple homicide, but now just for questioning," Ebony explained.

Kash pondered everything, then asked, "You got a number on him?"

"No, he called me private," replied Ebony.

"Ok, so how are my kids and you?"

"Getting big. They missing you, though. How are you doing?" Ebony was concerned.

"Yeah, I'm good. So do you know the plan he got going on?" Kash asked, still lost about what Ebony just told him. What had happened to make Gangsta just snap was the question he needed to know.

"No, he just said he had a plan and that he will keep me updated. Right now it's a manhunt for him, so I don't think he gonna contact me just now."

"Ok, cool. Well, I love y'all. And expect a letter from me. I will call tomorrow, too. I need you to get me two $500. No ID. Pick up from Western Union," Kash told her before getting ready to hang up.

"Ok. We love you, and call tomorrow. By this time I will have that for you," his babymama replied, and they ended the call.

Kash walked to the door. He looked through the bottom to see if the officer was making his rounds, as the shift required. The coast was clear, so he called Erica's old number to find it cut off, then he tried Ne-Ne's. It went straight to voicemail. He was getting frustrated, with only twenty more minutes before his time was up on the phone. Kash had to think, and think fast. He didn't have Gangsta's mother's number. And the niggas in the hood, he definitely didn't have their numbers. He'd been in prison too long. Out of sight, out of mind.

Kash called Ebony back and told her to get a number on Gangsta, which she agreed to. He gave the phone back to the orderly when he pulled up. All Kash could do was sit back and see what this plan was Gangsta had up his sleeve. He so bad wanted to be out there, to have his brother back. He knew Gangsta could hold it down. He still needed his support.

Kash wondered who was responsible for shooting Gangsta's son. He knew Gangsta was going crazy over this, because he was one man who loved his son. Junior was Gangsta's pride and joy, and everyone who knew Gangsta knew this.

Kash lay back on the bunk. He picked his book back up to finish reading, but this time with a full mind.

***

Ne-Ne

She and Erica were in the waiting room, asleep, when they were woken up by a very pretty female in a business suit and heels. Ne-Ne focused her eyes and sat up straight in her seat. The woman was holding a folder. Ne-Ne noticed she had a gun on her hip, then Ne-Ne saw the badge with *FBI* written on it.

"Excuse me, Ms. Robertson, is it?" The woman was young and soft-spoken. She looked to be in her twenties.

"Yes," replied Ne-Ne.

"Ok. I'm Special Agent Williams on behalf of the government. We picked up your kidnapping case," the woman spoke while taking a seat next to both sisters. "And you must be Erica."

"I am," Erica replied. She held a questioning look on her face.

"I don't remember much. I already told this to the detectives," Ne-Ne added. Right now wasn't the time to be talking to the cops. She was more worried about her son.

"I understand, ma'am, but I'm not the detectives, and I'm not looking to lock anybody up on your side. I just want to hear your side of the story. And yours." The agent looked at both sisters, being as respectful as possible.

"Like I said, I can't tell you much," Ne-Ne replied, sticking to her story. Her sister caught on and went with the flow.

The woman took down both of their information. She was understanding and nice. Ne-Ne respected that, but at the same time she wasn't willing to help her, no matter how sweet she was.

"Well, can I ask the both of you to come into my office at your convenience to answer a few questions? I still have to make a report to the government. I am not trying to get on your bad side. I understand that you must be going through a lot right now." The agent stood.

Ne-Ne agreed to come down the very next day. She decided not to be as stubborn as she felt, because the woman did come with respect.

After the woman left, Ne-Ne walked down to the nurses' station to see if she could get an update on what was going on. Junior was still in surgery. It'd been sixteen hours. She wanted to know the progress. She saw Mrs. Jackson talking to an FBI agent, and Terry was in the hallway speaking to another agent. The situation had turned serious.

Ne-Ne noticed the head doctor was just walking out of the surgery room. She was headed to the waiting room area until she saw Ne-Ne and started in her direction. She wore a look Ne-Ne couldn't read.

"Ms. Robertson, come into my office, please."

She followed the doctor as requested. Her heart rate sped up in her chest as she thought of her son and any bad news. The office was tiny, but neat. Ne-Ne stood up while the doctor took her seat. She put both hands on the desk, clasped together, and looked directly at Ne-Ne before speaking.

"Ok, so this is what's going on. Surgery was somewhat a success. We didn't get far, but we got something. All your son's vitals have increased. However, he is still supported by the machine. He is still brain dead, and more surgery is required, but first we want him to heal up, rest some. We will watch his vitals and see if they increase any more before we try surgery again."

The information the doctor gave Ne-Ne was music to her ears. She felt so good hearing the news that a bright smile appeared on her face. "Thank you so much, Doc. Thank you!" Ne-Ne stressed her appreciation and also thanked God, because it was good will that kept Junior fighting for his life.

"No problem. So what we will do is give him two weeks to see if anything good or bad happens. He's a strong kid, a fighting soul, and to be honest, this is a first this has happened," the doctor said. She was also thankful that there was now a fighting chance for the baby. She was happy to add to Ne-Ne's joy.

Leaving the office, she went into the waiting area to share the news with her sister, then texted and told Gangsta exactly what the doctor said. She knew he needed to hear some good news about his son. It was late, so she didn't expect a reply. Ne-Ne pocketed her phone. She wanted to shed tears of joy, she was so happy at the moment.

"Come on, let's ask the doctor if we can see him." Erica took her sister's hand, also happy about the news.

Jerry Jackson

Chapter 14

FBI Agent Latrisha Williams

Her heels clicked loudly as she rushed down the hall, late for her meeting with Captain Oliver Brown. Sweat appeared on her forehead, as she was moving at a quite pace, not wanting to be even more late. The room was crowded with federal agents. When she finally made it and opened the door, her captain was standing behind a podium. He was in the middle of talking when she entered. The entire room turned to see her. The captain stopped speaking until she found her seat in the back.

"Welcome, Agent Williams. You only missed a small portion, so I will start over from the top," the captain spoke to her, looked down to his paperwork, then back up to the crowd. "Now, back to what I was saying. This operation has not been approved yet 'cause we do not have proper grounds to stamp it as a drug war. However, it doesn't stop us from running an investigation trying to find links and connections of these recent crimes. Agent Grace and Agent Marcello are assignment to the shootout on Hollywood Road. Agent Williams and Norris, you take the kidnapping case, since y'all have already started in that direction."

"So how do we do groups?" one agent asked from the front of the room.

"We will have two shift teams. Everyone report to the head, and please do not get out there and force something to make a case. We need to get the approval from front office before we can go to locking people up and charging them with crimes we think they did."

The captain clicked on the projector, and a picture of Bam popped up. The captain took a seat as another senior got up. It was the FBI Chief Director, Mrs. Mathis. She looked upon all the agents in the room, then picked up a ruler she pointed to the picture.

"We have reason to believe Bernard Gresham, AKA Bam, is linked into this circle some kind of way. A few days ago he lost our surveillance team. Disappeared right into traffic."

"Isn't he a government informant?" came a question from the back of the room.

"Yes, Bernard will soon testify for the government. He's been working with us a few months now," Mrs. Mathis addressed the questions. She clicked to another picture. It was a photo of a Mexican, an older, frail-looking man. His hair was full and white as snow, Latrisha noticed. "This is one of Mexico's top cartel leaders. His name is Mr. Play, and this," she clicked to another picture, "this is his son, Chavez, who runs the entire operation for his sick father." Mrs. Mathis clicked another picture. It was a clean-cut looking Mexican. He looked more like a business owner than a criminal. "His name is Loco. This is the son of Chavez. He runs the drug trade through Atlanta and Miami. All of this is assumptions, because we are still trying to get Bam to give up his connection."

"So, do we think that 'cause Bam turned informant, the cartel is after him and it's war?" someone asked out of the crowd.

"Safe to say, yes."

"Do we have locations on Chavez, Loco, and Mr. Play?" another agent asked.

"Chavez and Mr. Play boarded a private flight back to Mexico eight hours ago. Loco's time is mostly spent in Buford, Georgia. Intel got him at four different houses throughout Gwent County," Mrs. Mathis confirmed.

The meeting lasted another hour. Latrisha was taking down every note possible. This would be her first lead in an investigation. She was only twenty-nine years old. She had been with the force three years and was slowly making a name for herself with her quick wit and charm. She was very smart and driven. She loved her job and everything about it. She was there to prove herself to anybody who didn't believe she could make it up to the top. It was her pretty face and nice body that made people assume she was soft and too girly to be a federal agent. What people didn't know was that she came up in a rough neighborhood in Augusta, south side projects with some of the worst criminals she'd met. Latrisha was self-driven and has seen far past being in the hood with a dope boy for the rest of her life. True indeed, she liked the rough-around-the-edges type, but what she liked and what was important were two different things. She had a family to take care of, and if she didn't do it, then nobody would. So that was her sole reason for going to school, through college, and into the police force — Not because she wanted to be police, but for career choices.

Latrisha went to her office. She pulled the file up on Bam and began to read up on him, determined to figure this case out.

***

Gangsta

Gangsta and Loco were leaving the airport in College Park, seeing Chavez and Mr. Play off back to Mexico. During the ride to the airport, Chavez continued to vividly paint pictures of what it would be like to have Gangsta as their sole distributor in Atlanta. All Loco did was agree with a shake of his head each time his father made a point, and all Gangsta did was listen. He had a plan, but being an Atlanta drug dealer was well out of the door now. He would leave that position to the next person. Gangsta would be the sacrifice to his son's healing, just as his son was the sacrifice to his karma in the streets.

The deal Chavez was giving him was all that he, Kash, and Dank had ever wanted. This opportunity was the one they worked hard for, took many lives for. They hurt a great amount of people to see this day, but to Gangsta that dream had long died. All he wanted was revenge. It was more important than riches, so Gangsta's mind was already made up. But he wouldn't be a fool and just keep bluntly declining Chavez's offer. Gangsta finally told Chavez that he would work for him under one circumstance.

"Name it, my friend," Chavez said.

"Give me one week to get shit lined up and we got a deal," Gangsta said, looking across to Mr. Play and Chavez. This would be their last time seeing each other. Chavez just didn't know it. He would disappear on them without notice, and nine times out of ten never come back. Gangsta didn't want to do it like this, but if his plan was to work, then he had no other choice. Chavez wouldn't let him say no, Loco either, so Gangsta went with the idea, but really all he cared about was his son's well being. Nothing else mattered, not even his own life.

"We have a deal, my friend." Chavez smiled, then spoke to Mr. Play in Spanish, who in returned smiled at Gangsta with a nod of his head, happy Gangsta took the offer.

Gangsta and Loco made it back to Gwent, meeting up with Jeter and Longo at Melody and Mya's house.

"Way, I got business to handle that requires me to ride throughout the city limits. If you want, you can join me. Or do you have other plans?" Loco asked once they got out of the range rover and everyone dapped each other.

"Naw, way, I don't have no plans, but I'm good on riding. I'ma just chill here a few hours to collet my thoughts before heading out," replied Gangsta.

"Cool. Make yourself at home." Loco patted his back as they walked inside the house.

Mya was standing over the stove cooking when they entered the kitchen. Loco kissed his sister's face. She eyed Gangsta with a look he never noticed. Longo went to the already-done food and dug in. Mya playfully swung at Longo. He laughed, moving out of reach. Gangsta looked on and laughed at them both. Mya was looking good in tight jeans and a tank top. Her ass bounced with every step she took, he couldn't help but notice. Mya was one of them hip-hop types. She was into all the fashion and music, she knew all the slang and swagger. She acted as if she was black, is what Gangsta thought.

"Let's go, fellas," Loco announced ten minutes later after he had gotten situated. Loco was heading out the door.

Gangsta took a seat at the dinner table next to Longo, who wasn't playing with his plate of food, knocking off the last of it.

"Anything you need, my friend, just say the words. You know the number. I will be back in a few hours," Loco reminded him when he stopped before completely going out the door.

"Cool, way. I probably be here when you get back. However, if I'm not, it won't be long before I do show up," Gangsta said.

Loco left with Jeter and Longo, leaving Gangsta alone with this beautifully put together Mexican girl. Mya was bad, he had to admit, with a fat ass to go with her almost-perfect body.

She caught Gangsta looking at her while fixing him a plate of food. She didn't speak on it, and neither did he. Mya was most definitely a sight to see, and under different circumstances Gangsta would have been all over her, but right now pussy was the last thing he wanted. Right now, no matter how much he was lusting, he refused to give in to it. He had entirely too much business to handle.

The food was good, he had to admit, or he was starving. Mya had left him at the table when he went back for seconds. Gangsta took that time to make some phone calls. The first person he called was Nikki so he could get word on what was being said on the west side.

Nikki surprised him when she stated, "They got Poonie, charged him with all six murders and everybody that got injured."

"Damn, for real?"

"Yes, I'm going to visit him today," Nikki spoke.

"Fuck! You think shawty made a statement already?"

"I don't think so, but I don't know," replied Nikki.

"Ok, look, tell him I got the lawyer. Just sit back. He won't get convicted. Tell him I promise he won't. Check this out, though: I got a check for you and Roxanne for keeping it clean. I'ma drop something extra on you for Poonie, to hold him down 'til he bounce. Text me the address y'all at. I'ma pull up later." It was the least he could do for them, because they did help him along the way, and he respected them for that.

Gangsta finished his food, then headed to the spare room where his duffle bag was hidden in the closet. He grabbed it, pulled it out, tossing it on the bed. Gangsta pulled another cellphone out of his pocket. He sat on the bed and activated the phone. Gangsta was now moving forward on his mission. He had a ton of shit to put in place, making sure everything was on point. He had a bunch of people to involve in order to succeed in his plan.

After he had the phone activated, Gangsta sent a text to Bam's number.

Bitch-ass nigga you can't run and you not protected.

Gangsta cut the phone back off, took the battery out, and smashed the phone up. He had no more use for it.

Gangsta got up and tossed the duffel bag full of money and drugs over his shoulder. Reaching under the pillow, he grabbed a brand new .45. He removed the Beretta from his hip and placed it in the drawer with another gun and a chopper clip. When he stepped out of the room, Mya was standing in the hallway in a long t-shirt and he could only imagine what else. Gangsta looked at her. She looked at him. Neither said anything for a moment, but then Gangsta straightened up. He had to stay focused.

"You leaving?" asked Mya.

"Yeah. Got some business to handle," Gangsta replied and walked past her, saying, "Excuse me." Mya held a disappointed look on her face. He had to get out of there before he got off course, because he could be reading it wrong, but it surely looked like Mya was ready to be fucked. He jumped into the 442 Cutlass and found the highway. He was going to see Mr. Swinn.

Jerry Jackson

Chapter 15

Bam

He met Trina and her cousin with his crew at one of his warehouses on Fulton Industrial. Trina's cousin was a real hothead with a squad that call themselves Murder. His name was Coco, an east Atlanta rider, born and raised on Glenwood.

Bam took everyone into the warehouse. He heard a few mumbles and a couple deep inhales when they all saw Pam badly beaten, her guts hanging out of her stomach. As she was cuffed overhead, her hands were turning blue from no blood circulation because she was so weak she couldn't stand on her own two feet. Bam paid it no mind while taking a seat on the table, legs swinging. He looked the squad over for a brief moment, then he spoke.

"If you niggas not willing to die for this money, then you need to leave this place now. It's a war I'm in, and I plan on winning it however I gots to. Each of you cats will receive a fat bonus when this shit over with, and as long as y'all with me, you will be straight. So who is down, and who is not?" Bam got straight to the point. All the niggas with Trina's cousin said they were in, and that's when Bam gave them the layout on what he needed done. "Yo, and somebody finish that bitch off," Bam added while walking off. Trina followed close behind.

His phone vibrated in his pocket. He pulled it out to see a message from a number he didn't recognize.

Bitch-ass nigga you can't run and you not protected.

Bam stared at the number, then dialed it to get the voicemail. He knew it was Gangsta, then wondered if he knew about his house in Mount Zion. But if he did know, Gangsta wasn't stupid enough to bring war to his spot. And if he was that dumb, the Feds would for sure snatch him up. He wouldn't make it past the front door.

Bam wanted Gangsta badly, because now he was becoming a pain in the ass. Business had to continue. He was losing money as the days rolled around. He had to reorganize his go-to men with the blow or weed, but first thing first, he had to pick the right one to trust to handle business correctly.

Coco walked over to Pam's limp body. He lifted her head up. Both of her eyes were swollen shut, her nose broken, her lips busted, her jaw broken. She was fucked up so badly that Coco shook his head, disgusted. Then, with one vicious twist, he snapped Pam's neck, doing her a favor by killing her.

Everyone in the warehouse followed Bam to the back where crates of guns and ammo were piled up.

"All y'all niggas get a choppa and two hand guns. There's plenty ammo to go around." He watched as everyone strapped up, getting ready to light the west side of Atlanta up looking for Gangsta.

"Daddy, you know I will bust my gun, too, anytime you need me," Trina said out of nowhere, bringing his attention back from deep thoughts.

Bam looked at the message again. Just to be sure, he then sent a text back.

lol

"I know, shorty, but all I want for you to do is look pretty while yo' nigga handle his business, ok, Ma?" Bam pulled her into his arms. He kissed her neck, not trying to show her signs of him weak or worried, but Trina was a girl in love, which meant she was always passing attention to him and knew him better than he gave her credit for.

***

Gangsta

His black Atlanta Braves hat was pulled down low on his face, wearing a pair of Gucci frames to hide his true appearance, giving anybody who noticed him a different look from the pictures they saw on TV. Gangsta pulled the 442 up to Michael Swinn's law firm, located on South Cobb Drive, Cobb County. Every whip in the parking lot was expensive, he noticed, while taking the gun under his thigh and placing it in his waistband, concealed. Gangsta got out of the Cutlass, fresh in Gucci heavy black jeans, the black sweater with white trim to match, and a pair of snow white Tim's. He carried a tote bag inside the firm.

It was beautifully decorated when he entered. The air was clean and it smelled very nice, smelled like business. Gangsta walked up to the desk. A white female in her late thirties was on the phone. She smiled at him, then held up one finger for him to wait.

"I'm here for Swinn. Is he in his office?" Gangsta wasn't about to be put on hold, and the clerk saw it in his eyes. She hung up the phone.

"How are you today, sir?" Her voice was beautiful.

"Swinn. I'm here for him. Is he around?" he asked again.

"One second," the girl said, then picked up the phone and quickly hung it up after speaking with Swinn. She gave Gangsta a bright smile before saying. "He's waiting on you, sir."

"Thanks." Gangsta walked through the door marked with Swinn's name on it. He was seated behind his huge desk. His office was very large, the kind of office that held a bathroom, a coffee station, and had a sitting area with two leather sofas and a table.

"Gary, how are you?"

"I'm straight. What's up? What's going on with my case, though?"

Mr. Swinn sat upright in his seat. He rummaged through a stack of papers on his desk and found what he was looking for. Mr. Swinn took his eyeglasses from their case. He put them on, then he began reading from the paperwork.

"State was overridden by federal government, so it's them with your case now. And the status is still the same. You are just wanted for questioning, so I'm just sitting back, waiting for them to strike so I can defend," Mr. Swinn assured Gangsta.

Gangsta pulled the money out of the tote bag. He tossed four big stacks on the desk. "That's 200 racks, and this is what I need from you." Gangsta held a note up, then passed it to Swinn, who took it in return. He read the first couple lines, then looked up to Gangsta, skeptical.

"You sure about this?"

"I'm positive," replied Gangsta. Mr. Swinn continued to read from the paper. Now he was confused, because Gangsta was asking him to do what no man had ever asked.

The next place Gangsta went to was Ebony's crib after calling to make sure it was safe to come there. She said it was cool. Ebony didn't stay that far from the lawyer's office. Gangsta got there in fifteen minutes, driving with both windows down and seatbelt on, because Cobb County did not play games with dope boy cars and tinted windows.

Ebony was in her driveway when Gangsta pulled the 442 up behind her car. He left the cutlass running and jumped out. Ebony had a huge smile on her face. She hurriedly walked over to meet him.

"Brother, how are you?" She hugged Gangsta with pure intent. It was good to see him holding up.

"What's up, sis?" Gangsta returned the love. They both walked toward the house. "Where the kids?" he asked.

"With my parents. I'm in the process of moving." Ebony opened her front door and they both walked inside. Gangsta noticed the living room was empty. Only boxes decorated the large space.

"Oh, ok. You and Greg found a better place?" he asked and looked around.

The Streets Bleed Murder 2

"Unfortunately no, just me and the kids. Greg and I are going through a divorce. Long story. I will tell you about it later. What's going on with you, though?"

"Here." Gangsta gave her an address. "Her name is Ms. Griffin. She is the witness on Kash's case. And here," he gave her a folded paper. "I wrote down everything I need for you to do."

Ebony took everything he gave with a nod of her head that she understood. "I talked to Kash. He has a cell phone in there. Let me go write his number down. He is so worried about you." Ebony walked away to get a pen.

Gangsta smiled to himself because Kash always made shit happen, even in situations that seemed too impossible. It made Gangsta happy to know now he could talk to his peoples.

Ebony gave him the number, then just as quickly as he came, he left. Gangsta made it to the highway safe, bumping music while his mind wondered about his son. He needed to know how the surgery went, so he pulled out his phone and called Ne-Ne. she picked up with her normal tone of voice, not the agitated one.

"Hello?"

"What's up? Is surgery done?" he cut straight to the point. Since Ne-Ne was being extra with him, when he called or came around he decided to just let her have it at the moment. Indeed, he was still fully in love with her and she was the only woman that made his heart beat, but none of that mattered to him anymore. All that mattered to him was his son.

"Doctor's got to perform more surgery, but good thing is all his vitals have increased a bunch since the first surgery," Ne-Ne was happy to tell him.

"Is he still brain dead?"

"Yes, he still is, and on life support. This is all I've heard so far, but your mother said that things are looking up for our son." Ne-Ne sounded happy, and Gangsta liked that. He also felt good and silently thanked God for the work he had already started.

"Good, and what's up with you? Where are you? At the hospital?"

"I'm good, and actually I'm at your aunt's. We all decided to take some comfortable showers before going back to Grady," Ne-Ne replied, then asked, "How are you, though?"

It surprised him to hear that question.

"I'm good. Just lurking in these streets, you know," Gangsta shot back. "But yeah, I was just checking on Junior. I will get at you later, alright?"

He caught her off guard with that one. He heard it in her voice. "Ok, be careful, Gary." Ne-Ne was showing some kind of concern, something he hadn't seen in awhile, dealing with her.

"Yeah, I am," he replied, then they got off the line.

Gangsta gave God thanks one more time that Ne-Ne wasn't so harsh with her tone. He guessed Junior's status changing for the good was something to smile about.

Chapter 16

FBI Agent Latrisha Williams

"Regardless if you cooperate or not, you are going to prison. However, if you talk, you can get out sooner than a life sentence," agent Trisha Williams informed Poonie, who had yet to speak or write a statement. All they had was one witness, an old man who said he knew Poonie personally and said he looked like one of the shooters. Poonie couldn't believe Mr. Green had told on him after all the shit the hood witnessed Mr. green do with the young girls who were barley legal.

"We can help you, Poonie, but you got to help yourself. Six people was killed, a nine-year-old girl was shot, and at least four more people got hurt, so tell us: was this a drug deal going wrong or what? Who is who? Who is head?" Ms. Williams pressed, seeing she had Poonie's undivided attention with how he was looking at her chest.

"I don't know what y'all talking 'bout," was Poonie's reply. He had gotten a visit from Nikki telling him what Gangsta said he would do for him, so he wasn't about to get caught up with talking to the Feds.

"We have a witness to place you at the scene of the crime. That's all the government needs to place over ten violent crimes on you. Like I said before, I'm your best help, so you might as well play ball," Ms. Williams said again, but this time walking around the table, giving Poonie a view of her nice body. Men were weak like that. All a female had to do was flirt a little bit, show a little skin, and a man would forget his name.

"Like I said, I don't know nothing. Ask my lawyer is what you do." Poonie wasn't a snitch, and everyone knew that. Jail was no stranger to him. It was all good as long as Gangsta held him down like he promised he would. Poonie was willing to ride it out.

"I don't see how young men can just throw their life away at the drop off a hat. You have what? Two kids who are not important, right? We have a witness saying it was you who did most of the shooting. You do not have to take all this wrap by yourself," the agent said, looking across at Poonie.

"I wasn't shooting."

"Ballistics says you were. Ok, what about some of the guys' names that was against you? Could you tell me that? Living or deceased, it doesn't matter," she asked. leaning on the table.

"Listen, lady, I just told you I'm not the nigga you looking for. I'm the wrong guy. When you picked me up, I was at my mother's house, chilling. Did it look to you like I was in a fucking war? That's them lil' gang members. I'm too old for gangs or games." Poonie looked the agent up and down. He wasn't breaking. He wasn't talking.

"How old are your kids?" she asked.

"Grandparents, if y'all convict me for something I didn't do. I'm pretty sure you will find your man, though, because I'm not him."

That statement made the FBI agent mad. He could see the fire in her eyes as she gathered her paperwork and stood to leave. She looked down at Poonie, determined to nail him and all who was involved.

"Smart mouth, I see. Well, sir, let me let you in on a little secret." She bent down to his ear and whispered, "I'm federal government. We always win."

And with that said, she left Poonie in the interrogation room. Trisha was heated, but she still had to be professional with her approach to others. She had more interviews today. While walking down to her office, she dug inside her purse, looking at her phone to check for any calls, but saw none. Trisha knew her biggest lead would come from the Robertson girls who promised to meet her today, so that's where her hope stood.

***

Kash

Mad wasn't the word once he found out what was going on with Gangsta. Kash was heated that they didn't have a team to handle this situation. He knew Gangsta must be feeling helpless out there alone, going through this shit with his son. Any man would be going nuts if it was them in Gangsta's shoes. Kash knew himself. He would be killing any nigga that looked like Bam or even looked like they knew Bam. *The game is crazy,* he thought while working out in his tiny room, trying to ease the stress that had him by the ankles. He wanted to be there so bad with his friend, to have his back. Just the thought made him wish that bitch-nigga Dank would die in jail, or that he could get just one more chance to war with that nigga, just one more shot, and this time Dank would not be so lucky.

Kash was doing push-ups when his phone vibrated under the pillow on his bunk. It was a phone he bought from Meco's plug for 500. He did the last of his push-ups, then got up from the floor. He took out the phone to find a message from Ms. Berry, the CO who worked at Smith. She had sent some pictures, like he requested. Kash smiled at the mere sight of her and saved them to his phone. He sent her a nice little text, then finished working out before the showers started being run. It was shower day. In the hole in prison, they got three showers per week: Monday, Wednesday, and Friday. Kash wondered what would be Ms. Berry's reply to his question of them hooking up.

It took him another hour to finish and prepare for the shower. Since he was on high max, it took two officers to escort him to one of the shower stalls. Kash made sure to have his phone with him, wrapped up in his towel inside his net bag tossed over his shoulder.

"Fifteen minutes, McCants," one of the COs said when Kash was secured inside the shower and the door was locked. He still wondered what Gangsta's plan was with this lawyer stuff. What could possibly happen but a bunch of court dates and motions? It had been a moment since he'd seen the streets. Just the thought of being free again made him nervous. Kash didn't have a plan because he was sentenced to life in prison, but now Gangsta had something going on, something that could only be good.

The shower was quick and he was placed back in his room. Kash waited until the officer left before he pulled his cellphone out and powered it up. He tossed it on the bed and started putting on deodorant and the necessary things to get fresh. The phone started constantly vibrating, meaning it was someone calling. Kash picked it up.

"Yeah?"

"Whoa, what's hap', foo'?" Gangsta's voice said, which made Kash sit down on the bed, glad to finally hear his partner, his brother, his best friend.

"Nigga, what's up? You ok, bruh? What's going on out there, shawty?" Kash wanted to ask a million questions.

"Shit rough, shawty. This nigga Bam tried me, tried to kill da kid, but failed. And now the bitch-nigga running for his life, tucking his tail. My son on life support because of this nigga, bruh."

"Why the nigga try you though, foo'?"

"Shawty, I wouldn't fuck with that lame, and he got mad 'cause I didn't take up a six-man hit for him and Zay's bitch-ass, so the nigga had wifey door kicked in. Long story short, it went down in a major way," Gangsta explained.

"So what's up with this lawyer shit? You got me going to court and all. What's up?" Kash wanted to know.

"We trading places, bruh. My sacrifice, your freedom. You 'bout to be free, my nigga, and it's finna be laid out for you out here when you do."

"Da fuck you talking 'bout, foo'? I'm confused. What sacrifice?" Kash stood up.

"Bruh, you trust me, my nigga?" Gangsta asked.

"It's not 'bout that—"

"Bruh, do you trust me?" Gangsta cut him off.

"With my life, my nigga, you know this," Kash admitted.

"Well, my sacrifice, your freedom, foo'. So get ready to take over this shit I'm laying out for you. Love you, foo'. This my line, so lock me in and we'll talk some more later," Gangsta said.

Kash sat back down, shaking his head because it wasn't enough information. It wasn't what he was looking for. He really didn't want to let Gangsta end the call, but he had the number now.

"Say no mo', foo'. Love ya, too."

Jerry Jackson

Chapter 17

Gangsta

He was sitting inside the 442, watching the nurses and doctors come and go as the day turned into night. Gangsta was waiting for the right one to approach before he showed his face. He had to use his judgmental eye, his common sense, his street smarts before pulling up on anybody. His face still was on every news channel, his name was fresh in every radio host's mouth, so Gangsta had to be extra careful not to alert the cops by approaching either a nurse or doctor who would get scared and scream versus help him, as he needed the help. He had a lot on his plate to deal with, but not seeing his son was eating him alive. He had to see his lil' man one way or the other, then he could continue his plan.

Life was hard for him. Gangsta was losing it day-by-day, trying desperately to remain sane, not knowing who to trust, who to go at, or where to start. But first things first, he needed to see Junior.

Gangsta noticed one particular nurse climbing out of her car with a phone glued to her ear. She had a colorful hairdo and Air Max Nikes on with her scrubs, rings on most of her fingers. This meant only a few things: she was ghetto, a dope boy's girlfriend, or was just into fashion. Either way, this was the one. Gangsta would try, do or die. He smoothly got out of the cutlass and caught up with her before she entered Grady.

"Excuse me. Excuse me, Ms. Lady. Lemme holla at cha," Gangsta said and she stopped, looking at him up and down, then to his face again.

"What's up?" was her reply. Gangsta instantly peeped the hood in her. She even wore colorful contacts in her eyes. She was looking as if she recognized him, but it didn't matter no more.

"Ms. Lady, I need your help. I got a nice check for you to sneak me in to see somebody—"

"Oh hell no! You wanna try to kill a motherfucker in here? Hell naw!" She was trying to walk off, but Gangsta stepped in her path. "No, listen, it's not like that. It's a family member I'm trying to see, and I know visiting hours are over," Gangsta pressed. "Honey, do I look like Boo-Boo the Fool? I'm not new to this. I'm not slow, and I'm definitely not about to jeopardize my job for a total stranger," she said, about to walk around him, but failed when Gangsta grabbed her hand.

"All bullshit to the side, my son in there on life support, Ms. Lady. I'm that nigga on the news everyday." Gangsta pulled the Gucci frames off his face and removed his hat. "If you was a parent, then you would understand. All I want, shawty, is to see my son, give him strength, pray with him, just lend my support. A father's support. Here, I got ten grand to get me in there for twenty minutes, that's it." Gangsta was nearly begging. He pulled out a fat wad of cash. He pushed it toward her, but the nurse looked down to the money, then back to Gangsta's face. She now knew who he was, and the fear quickly spread across her face. She took a step back.

"Uh, I'm— I'm sorry, but I can't h—"

"Please, Ms. Lady. My son dying in this place. Just tell me how to get in without being noticed and don't put the police on me. You can have the money."

"I don't know. I need my job."

"And I know this. Just like you said, you not new to this. You know how to maneuver, so help a brother out, baby girl, please." Gangsta would hate to force his way. His mother worked here, so the last thing he wanted was to make a scene at her workplace. But if she saw Gangsta here, she would probably faint, and he didn't want that either.

The nurse had to see the desperation in his eyes, because she took the money, stuffed it into her bag, then said, "I got kids myself. I pray this don't backfire on me."

"In and out, I promise," was his reply.

"Come on. Just follow me, and put your disguise back on. It makes you look different, 'cause I didn't have a clue who you was, honey. Make sure you stay on my heels," the nurse said, and they both entered Grady.

It was crowded like every other hospital with people coming and going, crying and joyous, doctors, nurses, cops, and whatever else filled the place, making it easy for him to blend in as he and the nurse got on the elevator. He was kinda nervous because if seen by the wrong person — or worse, the cops — then it would go down in a major way, a way he did not want to see.

The nurse led him to the sixth floor. "Wait in here until I come walking past, then just follow me, ok?" She took him to a waiting room. Gangsta didn't trust it, but there was really nothing he could do but comply. The nurse saw him hesitant. "I just got to clock in and play normal. Don't worry, I'm not the police."

"How long I got to wait?" Gangsta was looking around to see if he saw the cops anywhere. The ICU floor was nearly empty because visiting hours were over.

"Two minutes, tops. You have trusted me thus far, might as well keep trusting," the nurse said, then walked off, leaving Gangsta without a chance to reply. He watched her closely, seeing her vanish down the hall and around a corner. Gangsta left the waiting room. He walked in the opposite direction, into another waiting area that had two people there, both laid across the chairs asleep. Gangsta stood halfway in, halfway out of the threshold, giving him a clear shot to see the nurse so if she did alert the cops, they would go the wrong way and he could make an escape as fast as possible.

Her two minutes turned into five, and Gangsta was getting worried now, feeling like the police were on their way. He was strapped, so he was prepared to shoot his way out of this place. But that was not the plan, and it would take every ounce in him to pull a trigger on the cops — or better yet, the heroes.

Gangsta's mind was thinking so much negative that he almost missed the nurse when she appeared and walked into the waiting room she left him at. She quickly came back out to see him headed her way. She smiled, shaking her head.

"I feel you. Come on, follow me." She led him down the hall, passed a couple rooms, then they stopped at a door. The nurse looked left, then right. "Twenty minutes. You got twenty minutes. I will be back. The doctors will make rounds in a while, so make it quick, please."

"Bet that," Gangsta replied while walking into the room, leaving her at the door.

It was dark when he walked in. Only the blue lights from the machines gave the room a glow. A nightlight plugged into the wall brightened a corner of the room where many bears, toys, and balloons sat. Gangsta slowly approached the bed. His son was hooked up to so many tubes, half his head covered up by a breathing masked over his mouth and nose. He was so tiny, so helpless, so peaceful. Gangsta broke down silently as he reached out to touch his baby boy's tiny hand.

"Just hold on for me, lil' one. We're strong, and we don't give up, you hear me? You a fighter, son, so keep fighting. I'm sorry I wasn't there to protect you, son. I'm sorry that this happened to you, but I promise to make them pay who is responsible. Just bear with me, son, please, ok? Daddy loves you. Your mother loves you. We all are waiting for you to open your eyes and smile that smile you got. Please get up, baby. Please." Gangsta dropped to one knee as tears fell fast down his face. He couldn't help it. He was crying so much that his stomach felt empty and his head began to hurt. Gangsta closed his eyes and prayed.

God. Lord God, please grant me this prayer in the fastest way possible. Take my life for my son's. Please heal him now, God. I'm willing to do anything for this miracle, God, just name it. I will put this gun down, I will change my whole life, I will do whatever it takes to see my son open his eyes again, to see him living life. God, you know that this was never my intention and that I was only trying to make a way for my family. I know I've did things that can't be forgiven. I have taken people's lives that deserve to live, and as a man, I admit to these things before you. I own up to all my wrongs, God. Just please spare my son. You said all I need is faith, God, and that I have, so what's next? God, please.

Gangsta's pride had gone out the door. He was broken and needed to be fixed. He rose up from the floor, bent down, and kissed Junior's mask, then wiped his face before heading to the door.

He stopped then. Reaching into his pocket, he pulled out his son's favorite toy: a mini bunny that hopped around. Gangsta placed it on the counter next to Junior's other gifts. He kissed his son once more, then left as promised.

The hallway was clear when he stepped out. The nurse and he made eye contact. She nodded, he nodded, and they walked away. Gangsta took the elevator downstairs. He got off and quickly got out of Grady.

He met up with Monkey at Magic City Strip Club in the VIP section. Loco had called him, telling him that word was Lucky, another New York nigga, was in town, and every time he was in town, he and Bam hooked up. Loco said Lucky's favorite club was the Blue Flame, so that's where he had Monkey, watching the scene until he got there. Gangsta made sure to stay low, just in case Bam popped up or anybody wanted to play Superman. he was for sure strapped. He gave the bouncer $500 to get in with his gun. The music was blasting as dancers slowly filled the VIP section, trying to catch a sweet lick tonight from all the top-notch ballers in the city. Gangsta just ordered two drinks, one for himself, one for Monkey.

"What's the word on your peoples, your son?" Monkey asked, sitting back in the comfort of the leather seating. He slid his gun out and laid it under his lap, inconspicuous to everyone but Gangsta. Gangsta did the same.

"He making it, shawty. Keep your eyes open. I'm not playing with this nigga tonight. If he shows up, I'm rushing head-first to this fuck-nigga," Gangsta said and meant every world. Bam would die tonight if he showed up as expected, like Loco said he would.

"I'm on every door. I been in this bitch since the doors opened, bruh. I ain't seen this nigga yet, but it's a heavy load of New York niggas in the cut that been here a few hours before you showed," Monkey said, turning up the drink Gangsta gave him.

"My people told me Bam 'posed to be meeting his mentor here, so I take it them his folks. But fuck them niggas, shawty. I'm ready to die 'bout mines. Bam's ass gon' get it, and I don't give a damn who don't like it," Gangsta stated, only taking a tiny sip from his cup.

"That nigga over there must be Bam's folks. He had nearly all the hos in his area, popping all types of bottles." Monkey nodded his head in the direction of a light-skinned dude, kinda heavyset, with long dreads. He was sitting alone, surrounded by four of the club's baddest females with not a care in the world. Gangsta really didn't know if the guy's name was Lucky or not. There was a lot of niggas balling tonight. He wasn't sure who was who.

"Might be," replied Gangsta, still looking. He saw one of the girls get up from where the big dude was seated. She was smiling from the dude saying something to her, smacking her ass in the process. She walked toward the exit of the VIP room.

Gangsta smoothly re-tucked his gun and got up to catch her. He was moving through people swiftly until he was right on her heels. He reached out and touched her arm. The girl turned around and instantly looked Gangsta up and down. She put on a smile.

"Where you sitting at? I gotta go freshen up, then I will be with you," she patted his chest.

"Shawty, I don't want no dance. This Gangsta. I need to holla at you," he said, and that's when the girl looked harder, surprised to see him again after he was all over the news.

"My goodness. What's up? Um, come on, follow me." Asia took his hand and led him to the back. They ducked off into the men's bathroom really quick. There were a few dudes inside who gave Asia the eye and Gangsta an approving look as they all filed out, one by one. Gangsta pulled her into the stall.

"You know that nigga in VIP you was just with?" He got straight to the point, no time to waste.

"Yeah, that's Lucky. He come down twice a year to party. He from New York, and between me and you, he's a king pin. I already know how you get down, so I advise you to not mess with that one, but there's plenty more niggas in here I can put you on." Asia had always seemed like she was down for him, since the first time they met.

"I'm good on that, lil' ma. I'm just trying to be sure I know who is in here. So do you remember that New York nigga Bam?" Gangsta liked her heart

"Yeah. Bam had reserved seats tonight, but canceled at the last moment. Him and Lucky party here together when he in town. What's up? Is everything straight?" Asia wanted to know, because now she saw Gangsta in a different form. Now she felt the tension in the air. She knew something was going on.

"Hell naw, lil ma. I'm tryna find this nigga Bam and murder him," Gangsta said low when he heard someone enter the bathroom. Asia shook her head in understanding. Gangsta nodded his head toward the stall door. She got the hint, and they both walked out. One of them New York niggas was pissing. He looked over his shoulder at Gangsta and Asia, hugged up and walking back out into the club. She leaned over to Gangsta's ear and spoke loud enough for him to hear her.

"I told you before that I want to be down. My offer still stands, so if you need me to play my part, just give me the blue print."

Her words caught him off guard. He was not expecting her to say that, but he did like what he had heard. Gangsta stopped, looked down at her, then said, "I'ma put you in my Will, lil' ma."

Gangsta hugged her and walked back into the VIP section, where Monkey had two girls dancing for him. Gangsta took a seat. He now had to come up with another plan. If Bam wasn't showing up, then being in the club was for nothing. One moment Gangsta thought to approach Lucky, but decided not to. He just sat back and watched who he thought was watching him.

Chapter 18

Bam

When Bam and Trina pulled up to his mansion, he wasn't surprised to see the Feds there, but he was surprise to see two vans and more agents. When the Benz pulled up, two of the agents rushed over. One snatched the back door open.

"Gresham, I should have you arrested for eluding my staff assigned to watch you," the FBI woman spoke. She was beautiful, Bam noticed as he got out of the Benz followed by Trina, who gave the lady an ugly look with her eyes.

"Ma'am, I haven't done anything that should put me in jail. It was your staff who got lost. See, I'm the leader, and it's their job to follow. I can not do them both," Bam said, smiling down at the young agent. She had to be a rookie. She didn't look like she could even be a desk cop in a regular police department, let alone a government federal agent.

"Play dumb," she said, then turned to a few of her fellow agents. "Search him and the car."

"Yo, hol' up. Is this allowed?" Bam protested, but was already prepared for a shakedown. He already knew that they would be waiting, just not as many as it was. But he and Trina were clean as a newborn baby. Bam was smart. He was far from stupid and always stayed two steps ahead of the game. The Feds were the reason he didn't go out to meet up with Lucky tonight. Instead, he sent his love through Coco and had Coco's squad combing the west side streets looking for Gangsta, wrecking anything that he was a part of.

Two of the agents grabbed Bam while the other ones got Trina and the driver. They were checked, then Trina was allowed inside the mansion with the driver. The Feds held Bam outside to question him of his whereabouts.

"In the past thirty-six hours, where have you been?" the pretty agent asked Bam.

He was leaning against the hood of his Benz. He wondered where she came from. He never saw her when he was dealing with the Feds, and seeing her now made him wish he did get the chance to meet her before this day. Bam smiled down at the beauty with lustful thoughts.

"I been with my lawyer, and most the time I was sitting in the library, you know, working on my case," he lied with a straight face.

"Liar. What library?"

"Forgot. Just ask my lawyer, ma."

"I'm not your fucking mother. I will see to it that you do not leave this house again. See, since you been in hiding, all types of crime have happened. And now that you have showed up, these crimes have stopped, apparently. Bernard Gresham, you are on restricted house arrest. You are not to leave these grounds for any reason at all. Failure to comply will land you in a cell until trial is over, you got that?"

The FBI agent was mad, he noticed, but truly didn't give a fuck. This situation was almost over, then he would be free. So as of right now, he had to let her have it.

"I hear you, shorty." Bam stood upright, about to walk around her. She stepped in his face.

"I'm not your shorty, either. I'm Agent Williams, the one who is desperately trying to put you in jail when you slip, so play with it," she said, then allowed him to walk away into his crib. Bam laughed to himself. *Bitch, I already worked my deal. Fuck you,* he said to himself, leaving them to the slam of his large door.

"What's up with them pussy-ass police, Daddy?" Trina was clearly mad. She jumped to her feet when Bam entered the house.

"Them hos just mad we jammed on them for a couple days. Fuck them, ma. Don't stress it." Bam pulled her into his arms. He kissed the top of her head.

"Yo, if you want to leave, you good, son. Me and shorty, we here for awhile," Bam told his driver, who stood at the door waiting for instructions. Bam needed the rest anyway, plus more thought time. Lucky had just dropped a load on him that he hadn't even seen yet, plus his connection in Texas wanted his money from the bails of loud he sent, because usually it took Bam three days to move the work — either weed or crack — but since this situation with Gangsta he'd been off schedule, and money wasn't adding up because he really didn't have nobody to put the work on. Bam was hoping Coco stood up to his expectations, because if so, then he would be the man in Atlanta. Trina needed to be right about her cousin. Though until Coco proved himself, Bam had some business to handle in finding those to push his product.

"Ok, boss. Just call if you need me," his driver replied.

Bam and Trina took the elevator up. He pulled his phone out to check its call log. Nobody important had hit him. Bam was glad his kids were picked up and were now in New York with family. Nothing else mattered to him now down in the south. He wasn't worried about his people being hurt because of his actions. Now he could go at Gangsta with everything he had, and he intended to do it.

"You want a shower, Daddy?" Trina asked once they reached the master bedroom. Bam flopped back on his king-size bed. He let out a deep exhale, ran his hand over his face.

"Yeah, ma, that's what I need. Some warm water and some warm pussy afterward," Bam said.

"This pussy hot, Daddy, and you know I got you," Trina replied. She climbed on the bed and straddled him. She removed his hand from his face, then bent down. They kissed as she rolled her hips, pushing her pussy down on his semi-hardness. Bam gripped her ass, then ran his hand up her back.

"Don't tease me, ma." Bam met her hip roll with his own, his dick now harder than a brick, ready to beat her guts in. Trina raised up, bit her bottom lip. Looking down at the man she was crazy about, she pulled her shirt over her head, tossed it to the floor, then removed her bra, revealing a full pair of firm breasts. He grabbed a handful, then tried to rise up to suck one of her hard nipples, but Trina pushed his head back, making him stay laid out on his back. She stood up over him and pulled down her jeans. He helped her by pulling them down, too. When they got down to her calves, Bam ran his hand up the back of her thigh. He now was sitting up. He kissed the front of her thigh, then with one swift motion he flipped her over on her back. He kissed her flat stomach as he pulled her pants over her feet, tossing them over his shoulder. The gesture made Trina laugh a bit, then Bam removed his own shirt. He got up off the bed and took his pants off.

"Scoot to the end of this bed, ma," he said, dick harder than it'd ever been. Trina complied by sliding down to the edge of the bed. Bam opened her legs and kissed her inner thigh, then looked at her pretty pussy with its fat pussy lips. He kissed her there. Then, spreading her lips, he drove his tongue into her love box.

"Shit, Daddy," Trina said from the warmth of his tongue.

Bam sucked her clit into his mouth, then circled the tip of his tongue over it lightly. Trina was rolling her hips to meet his efforts. Bam started to suck her clit in and applied more tongue pressure. He had her moaning left and right as she gripped his bald head.

"Oh, Daddy, don't stop," she moaned, and Bam flicked his tongue over her pussy lips, pulling them into his mouth between his lips, then rolled his tongue flat over her whole pussy.

Trina squeezed his head with her thighs as cum began to burst through her. Bam opened her legs back. She arched her back as he slipped a finger into her, then got back on her clit.

"Shit, Daddy! Fuck!" She was coming hard.

Bam lifted up after she calmed down some. He moved up between her thighs and slid into the tightness of some good, young pussy.

Chapter 19

Gangsta

When he and Monkey were leaving the club, Gangsta saw the dude from the bathroom watching him while on his phone. He followed them through the club, from the back to the front, letting it be known he was onto them. Gangsta tapped Monkey to put him on point about the situation at hand. Monkey instantly caught on. Looking over his shoulder, Monkey saw two more dudes cutting through the crowd. Gangsta and Monkey clutched their tools, ready to pop shit off.

"What's up, bruh?" Monkey wanted to know what Gangsta wanted to do, because he was ready for whatever. They made it outside the club.

"Fuck this," Gangsta said, turning around, face-to-face with the New York nigga as he approached. "What's up, nigga? You motherfucking following me?" Gangsta wasn't about to keep playing with these niggas. Anybody could get it right now.

The dude was caught off guard with that statement. He stopped a short distant from them. That's when Monkey recognized his face.

"Coco? What's up, shawty?" Monkey said. He had gone to school with Coco, and he was official, but that was only in Monkey's eyes, because Gangsta didn't know that nigga. The dude looked to Gangsta, then back to Monkey. His two friends also walked up. They all were standing in front of the club. The bouncers were out there as well.

"What's up, Monkey? You ok, my nigga? It's been a long time, huh?" Coco spoke and pulled his phone out to check its messages. "What y'all niggas 'bout to get into?" he asked, looking down at his phone. Gangsta peeped him texting someone, so he moved in a lil' closer, being more aggressive. He looked and saw Bam's number. Coco pulled his phone back.

"Fuck you doing, my nigga?" Coco pocketed his phone, now with his full attention on Gangsta. The other two friends were inching forward. Monkey quickly peeped the deal.

"Fuck you texting?" Gangsta said back, just as harsh.

"Huh?" Coco tried to play stupid. Gangsta looked around the parking lot. There were just a few niggas coming into the club, a crowd of people standing in front of the wing stand, and three bouncers. He looked back to the dude.

"Bruh, why you followed a nigga out the club?"

"Man, I just saw Monkey and—"

Gangsta lift the glock in a quick motion. Everyone moved with life-or-death speed. He let off two shots aimed at Coco's face, who ducked before Gangsta squeezed the trigga. The other two guys with Coco tried to make a mad dash to their car to get their guns, but Monkey wasn't having it. He ran both dudes down, shooting them both in the back, knocking meat from bones. Gangsta was at the corner of the club building, wrestling with Coco, who somehow got his hand on the gun. He was holding the barrel with one hand and Gangsta's wrist with the other. The three bouncers were stuck in fear. They wanted to help, but didn't want to fuck around and get shot in the process, so they called the cops. While the commotion was going on, Monkey walked over to both dudes and shot them both in the back of their heads. He ran back over to Gangsta and drew his gun.

Coco held his arms in the air over his head, preventing Gangsta from shooting him. Coco saw one of the bouncers. He screamed for help.

"Call the cops! Help me, man!" He was struggling under Gangsta's strength as Gangsta's hand was slipping loose. He kneed Coco in the nuts, catching him off guard, then he twisted his body. Coco's back was now against the building. Gangsta kneed him again. That's when Monkey hit Coco over the head with the gun, then he aimed the gun at Coco's face. He surrendered, letting the barrel of Gangsta's gun go, throwing his hands high in the air.

"Ok, Ok, you got it, bruh. You—"

Gangsta took a step back and aimed the glock directly at his face. He shot Coco twice between the eyes, sending his body crashing into the building, sliding down it. By now the bouncers had got the hell on. Gangsta ran to the 442. He and Monkey jumped in and smashed out of the parking lot and down the street.

"Fuck!" Monkey said, looking back as Gangsta did about eighty miles per hour down the streets. Now it was time to get away. They ended up jumping on the highway on MLK, headed to the south side.

"You good, nigga?" Gangsta asked while they flushed down 285.

"Hell yeah, I'm straight," Monkey replied, then Gangsta pulled his own phone out and called Loco, who picked up on the second ring.

"My friend."

"He was a no-show, way. Give me the address to Mount Zion. I'm going to end this shit once and for all, way. It's a headache," Gangsta said, only to get a pause first.

Then Loco said, "Way, do you think that's a good idea? I mean, the Feds are crawling all over his place, Gangsta. That's no good move, my friend."

"Good or bad, way, I'm going in."

"What about the plan we made with my father? All we have, my friend, is our word, so why would you abandon responsibility?" Loco asked, but Gangsta wasn't hearing him.

"Plan is the same, Loco. I got it, trust me. I'm just not walking these streets another day with Bam living, way. That's real talk, my friend."

"Way, the FBI is all over his home. He cannot leave. He is on restricted house arrest." Loco had intel on almost everything that happened in Atlanta.

"I can get in, way. I got this. Just text me the address, and then we can proceed wit' business." Gangsta wasn't taking no for an answer, and Loco finally gave in, even though he didn't want to. He

156

The Streets Bleed Murder 2

supported Gangsta's decision, because he understood the most important thing was Gangsta needing his revenge before anything else.

He and Loco got off the phone and, moments later, the address came through with a picture of the home. Gangsta looked over to Monkey.

"Bruh, I'm 'bout to drop you off, my nigga, 'cause this mission I'm going on is suicide, and you have done enough for me, my nigga. That's love, Shit got to happen tonight, do or die, bruh." Gangsta had his mind made up. With no plan, all he knew was that he was going headfirst, no stopping, murdering anything that was in his way.

"So, if you don't make it, I'm just out of the plug?" Monkey asked.

"I don't know what to tell you on that, bruh, but I'm not planning on losing," was Gangsta's reply.

"I feel you, but I done came this far. Might as well ride this shit out, bruh. I'm with you," Monkey informed. He was willing to take it there with Gangsta because he felt his pain, he saw the hurt in him, and Gangsta was a good nigga. Good niggas shouldn't go through that.

"Ok, bet that. Then, my nigga, I gotta make a run to get more ammo. I need to drop you somewhere a few hours, and we'll pull up in the wee hours of the night."

"That's cool wit' me," Monkey replied. Gangsta took him to a hotel close to Jimmy Carter Boulevard, then he made it out to Melody's house. He used the key given to him to enter. He walked inside. Mya was on the floor, counting money with the machine. Melody was coming down the steps.

"Hey, Gangsta," Melody spoke, then joined her sister on the floor.

"What's going on, y'all?" he spoke back. Mya waved and went back to work. "Where is everybody?" Gangsta was headed up the steps when melody replied.

"It's just us here. Loco is out on business."

When he made it upstairs, he went into the room and got the guns he needed. He stripped down out of his clothes and hopped in the shower really quick to wash that pussy-nigga blood off him. He felt kinda better, being that he had seen his son and that his condition was getting better, but the issue with Ne-Ne was still at hand. It bothered him, but it couldn't be his focus. And even after this situation was over, Gangsta knew that he and Ne-Ne couldn't be together anymore. No matter how much he was in love with her, there would be no them.

He made his shower quick, then got out. He was standing in his boxers when the door was opened and Mya walked in. She stopped when she noticed his ripped muscles and six-pack glistening from the water. Gangsta reached for his tank top first, looking at her. She was seemingly stuck.

"What's up, Mya? Is everything good?"

She walked further into the room, closing the door behind her. She looked back at the door, locked it, then looked to Gangsta.

"I never been with a man such as yourself." She walked closer to him. She reached out and touched his chest.

Gangsta smiled. He was flattered, but sex was the last thing on his mind right now, and Mya was for sure bad. She ran her finger down his stomach. Gangsta grabbed her hand to stop her.

"Loco ain't like—"

"Loco know me and Melody likes you, so don't throw him up. I just want to sample you, not lock you down. I know you stressing and got so much more going on than what I want, but you are here now, half naked, so let me help you ease that pressure," Mya said and reached for his dick, which by then had begun to get hard just by the words she spoke. She was aggressive, and it was cute.

"You're very demanding, you know?" Gangsta spoke as she reached into his boxers, freeing his member. It hung out semi-hard. Mya stroked it, surprised at the size of it. She squatted down and licked just the head. She looked at it, stroked it some more, then put it in her warm mouth. Gangsta had forgotten how good pussy and head felt as he began to brick up in her mouth. Mya sucked and stroked him. She pulled off the dick, lifted it up, and licked up the shaft of him. She suckled on his balls, which made Gangsta grab her head, nearly standing on the tips of his toes. A silent moan escaped his mouth. Mya put the dick back into her mouth and went down as far as she could, gagging a little. She pulled back, inhaled deep. She spit on his dickhead and went back to sucking and stoking him. Gangsta started gyrating his hips, fucking her pretty face. He pushed his dick down her throat twice, making her gag again, then he lifted her up by the chin.

"Bend over."

Gangsta turned her around. He pulled her tights down to her ankles. She had a fat ass. He took his dick at the base, then rubbed his dickhead between her warm pussy lips. Mya spread her legs wider as he pushed inside her tightness. She moved a little, but he wouldn't let her go too far.

"C'mere. Uh! Uh!" Gangsta slid into her and started pumping in and out. Mya gripped the sheets. Gangsta gripped her ass and went to work. It was soft, how his hands sunk into her fat ass. Her pussy was super wet. Mya was moaning and trying to run from his size, but Gangsta wasn't having it. He was in a zone.

They both climbed on the bed. She was now lying flat on her stomach as he pinned her down at the small of her back.

"Papi, no. No! Papi, take some out! Oh. Oh, papi!" Mya continued to try to slide up from him beating her guts. He was near his peek, so he laid flat down with her and started deep stroking, talking in her ear.

"Where you want this nut?" he asked.

"My ass, papi," she said back.

"Ask me where I want to put it." Gangsta dug up in her. She winched out in pain.

"Where, Papi?" she nearly yelled.

"In your mouth. I want you to taste me."

"Ok, Papi."

As soon as she said the words, Gangsta pushed up off her, holding his dick at its base.

"Turn over," he said, and she did as told. She flipped over on her back. Gangsta aimed his dickhead at her mouth. She opened up wide as he released his thick, white sperm.

It shot in her mouth the first time. The second load hit her chin. That's when she grabbed his dick and put her mouth over its head to catch the rest of him. She sucked like a vacuum cleaner, making Gangsta moan and shiver. He had to snatch his dick out of her mouth, feeling like she was draining the life out of him. Mya smiled and wiped the remaining cum off her chin, put it into her mouth, and swallowed everything he let out. Gangsta was on his knees, holding his limp dick, looking at the beauty laid on her back and looking at him

"Thank you, papi," Mya smiled and got up. Gangsta didn't reply. He only flopped down on his back, wishing he didn't give in to the lust that took over him, but it had already happened. He laid there another minute in thought, then finally decided to get up. He had business to handle.

When he made it back to pick up Monkey, he was dressed in all black, just like Gangsta. He got in the 442. There were two choppers on the backseat and a vest.

"Put that on, bruh."

"Cool. So, do you got a plan?" Monkey asked while reaching to grab the vest. Gangsta pulled off into traffic.

"Yeah, murder, I never been to this nigga's shit, so I guess we case the spot to see how the Feds are posted and we get around them. See, one thing I know is the Feds will not think, nor Bam, that a nigga would bring this drama to his front door." Gangsta jumped on the highway.

"I know, but what if it's a load of Feds? Then what?"

"Then we lay 'til the opportunity presents itself. Either way, bruh, it's going down tonight."

"Shid, I'm with you," Monkey replied as Gangsta's phone started ringing. He looked at the number and saw it was Kash. He picked up, even though he didn't want to.

"Whoa."

"Shawty, what's up?"

"Lurking, bruh. What's hap', foo'?"

"Officer told me I'm leaving tonight, going back to the county. Said my judge granted some out-of-time motion," Kash said, which made Gangsta smile and tap Monkey. He pointed to the rolled-up blunt in the cup holder.

"That's the move, shawty. You 'bout to hit these streets, my nigga."

"Bruh, I still want to know your plan, my nigga. When you gon' share?" Kash asked and laughed, because he, too, was happy at the thought of freedom.

"You gon' know, foo'. I'm not gon' say it just yet, but trust me, it's what you deserve, shawty," Gangsta said.

"I can dig it, bruh. I can't wait to get out and we take this shit over. I miss you, my nigga. Whatever you got going on, I know it's good, so I'm with you, shawty."

He and Kash talked a while longer, then Gangsta ended the call when he made it to Clayton County. It was now or never. The nervousness washed over him, then quickly passed when he thought of his son, his babymama, and all that Bam had taken him through. Gangsta parked the 442 at a shopping center and cut it off. He and Monkey smoked two blunts, listening to Monsta Swole.

"We walking to this nigga's spot, shawty, so we can get away and look normal when we just walking," Gangsta said once the blunts were over. He opened the door and got out to the night sky. It was almost 1:00 a.m., so most folks should be asleep.

"You ready, bruh?" asked Monkey.

"Yeah, let's do it."

The walk was ten minutes. They walked past so many big homes and finally made it to Bam's house. Gangsta was surprised, and so was Monkey, at how big it was, plus it was gated with cameras all over in every corner. There was no way possible for them to get past the gate that had to be opened from the inside. They walked down the street and still couldn't figure out how to get in without being seen by the many cameras, the Feds, or the neighbors. Gangsta wouldn't give up. He had to come up with another method, so he and Monkey made the ten-minute walk back to the car.

"Let's go eat real quick," Gangsta said.

They jumped back into the 442. He was not that hungry, but he needed somewhere to put his thoughts in order, because this was the last shot. Gangsta knew that tonight he might die, so the move he made had to be his best shot.

They ate at the Waffle House, went inside and got seated. Monkey instantly picked up the menu. A waiter walked over.

"How are y'all today? You ready to order?" She was a white girl with a beet-red face and long, curly hair.

"No, not yet. Bring us some water, though," Gangsta told the girl, and she left.

"You think we can jump that fence?" It was a random question that came out of nowhere.

"Fuck no," was Monkey's stiff reply. "We might as well ram the gate if we gon' do that."

While Monkey was talking, Gangsta noticed a familiar face, but really couldn't place it. He was seated at the bar, having drinks in a business suit. Gangsta stared so hard that Monkey looked back over his shoulder to see what had Gangsta's attention. "What's up, bruh? What you see?"

"That nigga over there look like I know him." Gangsta pointed on the low.

Monkey then saw who he was talking about. His eyes got big. His voice low, he reached across the table and touched Gangsta's arm. "Boy, that's one of Bam's drivers," Monkey said, excited.

Gangsta looked out to the parking lot and spotted the Benz, which confirmed the dude was indeed Bam's people.

"Oh, we finna snatch him up," Gangsta said. He watched the dude eat his fresh food and flirt with the waiter. Monkey and Gangsta ordered their food also. He never took his eyes off the dude, not for one second, because this was the closest he would get to Bam. Right now, Gangsta needed the Benz, because it would get them past the gate, and all he needed was to get in. Another couple minutes and the dude was about to leave. Gangsta got up and so did Monkey, leaving no tip. The driver was oblivious, walking toward the Benz when Gangsta ran up behind him, pushing the gun into the small of his back.

"Die today or live forever, nigga. Open the door," Gangsta demanded to him as Monkey walked up, smiling and standing at the passenger door.

"Man, what's going on? You can have the money." The driver was shaken. The parking lot was empty. Not many people were out, and those that were really weren't paying attention to what was going on at that moment.

"Nigga, open the motherfucking door." Gangsta nudged the gun in the small of his back. The dude reluctantly complied. Gangsta made him unlock all doors, and Monkey got in, also with his gun drawn. Gangsta climbed in the back, glad that the driver didn't buck.

"Crank up and pull off, fuck-nigga," Monkey said, aiming the gun at his side.

"Listen, man. I'm just the typical nine-to-five worker, bruh. This car not mines, my nigga. Y'all can have what lil' money I got, but please, man, spare me my life," the driver pleaded.

"Bruh, crank this motherfucking car up. I'm not tryna rob or kill you, nigga, so don't make me. I want your boss man, nigga, and you my passport into the gates," Gangsta said.

"Feds are there. That's not a good idea," the driver warned him, but Gangsta didn't give a rat's ass who was there. With how he was feeling, he and Bam could both die tonight.

"Nigga!" Monkey reached over and choked the driver with one hand, pointing the gun with the other. "Crank this car."

"Ok, ok," the driver said and did as told. He cranked the Benz and pulled off.

"Now listen, you said you want to live, right?" Gangsta spoke from the backseat.

"Yes, I wanna live. Bruh, pl—"

"Listen, nigga. Shut up and listen. How many Feds there?" Gangsta was formulating a plan to attack.

"When I left it was two vans there, but usually its one or two cars, at least 'bout four agents."

"Do you got keys?"

"Yeah, I got keys. But man, I don't want to be a part of this stuff. I just want to quit right now," the driver was panicking.

"Look, if you want to live, I'ma let you. But check this, you gon' get me in that house. We just finna walk right past the FBI, go straight in."

"Man, that nigga might scream, bruh. Then we will murder some Feds," Monkey cut in. "Anyway, I didn't see no fuckin' vans when we went. It's just a couple whips in the driveway," Monkey said, and he was right, because Gangsta didn't see any vans either.

"We finna see. I'm just glad this bitch tinted," replied Gangsta as the Benz pulled up to the gate. It automatically opened, then the Benz eased through.

Gangsta was glad to see only one fed car with both white dudes standing in jeans and tucked-in blue shirts. They had guns on their hips and were leaned against the car.

The driver pulled up in his designated spot. "Now what?" he asked.

"We all gon' get out and walk toward the door. Monkey, me, and you gon' get the drop on them with the tool, 'cause they ain't gon' be expecting it. You gon' strip them and cuff them," Gangsta said and was the first to open the door, leaving nobody room to protest his plan.

Once his feet hit the pavement, it was all action, no flexing. Monkey and the driver did the same. Everyone looked normal walking toward the walkway leading to the doors. The Feds were posted there as well, looking at the three approaching. Gangsta became instantly nervous, but quickly killed it when he pulled his gun out. Monkey did too, more fearful, but ready to kill. The two federal agents were so caught off guard that they both just looked at each other, then back to the two gunmen.

"Don't move. Put yo' hands high in the air," Gangsta said, low. He knew he was taking a chance being out here like this with Bam having cameras and all, but it was a chance worth taking. The agents did as told.

"Go," he sent the driver. He took both the guns and the radios.

"Bring that shit over here. Sit it down. Go get them cuffs," Gangsta demanded, and the driver did as told. "I'm not gonna hurt nobody. I'm just going to see a man 'bout a mule, that's it. I'm in and out," Gangsta informed the agents after the cuffs were placed on them. He sat them down on the curb, then searched their car for guns and more cuffs. He found some and cuffed the driver to then, checked the agents' ankles for guns, and found that they both were strapped. He took the guns, laughing.

"Come on, shawty." Monkey and Gangsta headed into the house with the keys given. As soon as he got inside, Gangsta wished he would have gotten that nigga to tell him exactly where Bam slept. Both he and Monkey crept through the house, holding their guns ready to bust. Gangsta crept up the steps, Monkey on his tail. They made it upstairs and went room to room until they reached the master bedroom.

Gangsta slowly cracked the double doors, and he saw Bam. He burst through the door. Bam quickly rolled over with a gun in his hand, blazing heat in Gangsta's direction. He and Monkey ducked for cover while busting back.

By now Trina was up. She too had a pistol busting, giving Bam time enough to get on the other side of the bed. Gangsta picked her off with a headshot from a distance. Trina fell back and off the bed, her gun flying wildly in the air.

"Yeah, pussy-nigga," Gangsta said and started shooting in the direction of Bam while Monkey crept on the floor into the room more. Gangsta was in a rage. He was fearless and overall death-struck.

Gangsta stopped shooting when he noticed Bam's hands raised in surrender. Monkey had his gun directed at his face. Gangsta walked right over, pushed his gun to the side of Bam's face, and pulled the trigga, knocking brains out the other side. Bam fell sideways. Gangsta stood over his body and emptied the clip.

"Fuck-nigga." All types of emotions poured out of him as the gun erupted throughout the massive house. This was the day he'd waited for, the day he woke up every minute to see. Gangsta still was squeezing the trigga, even after the gun stopped busting. Only smoke escaped the barrel while he looked down at what once was Bam's face. Nearly everything was missing. All that was there was blood and bones. Gangsta spit on the body, then kicked what was left of its head.

He and Monkey made it back outside, glad to see the Feds and the driver were still cuffed. Gangsta looked at them while jogging to the Benz. He jumped in the driver's seat. Monkey hopped in the passenger's side. They pulled off, sparing three people their lives.

Chapter 20

Ebony

It was an early morning coming off a long night of watching the news and the worldwide manhunt for Gangsta. Last night he had murdered Bam and his girl in Bam's mansion. The shocking part to her was that Gangsta kidnapped the FBI agents. He was still at large, considered armed and dangerous, so the orders were to shoot on sight. Ebony was worried.

The news also said that someone else helped Gangsta, but they couldn't identify him at the moment, so mainly they wanted Gangsta. She had called his number, but it was off, so she made plans to go visit his mother after she handled the business with Kash and this lawyer. What Gangsta was doing for Kash, she appreciated him for that. It was something she would never even consider, but Gangsta was smart and she admired him for that.

Ebony pulled up to the address in Riverdale. She looked at the house, then into its driveway. Today she drove her squad car, even though she was off duty. Ebony climbed out with her gun and badge on her hip. All she could hope was that Gangsta's plan did not blow up in her face, because her job was on the line. Kash's life was on the line, too, and that was her reason for doing what she was doing. While she and Kash were not together, she still loved him and wanted to see him out because he was a great father to his kids, even with being as street as he was.

Ebony walked on the porch she knocked on the door, and moments later an older woman opened it.

"Ma'am, I'm Detective Morgan. How are you this morning?" Ebony asked as the lady gave her a skeptical look.

"I'm blessed. Yourself?"

"I'm looking for a Mrs. Murphy. Would that happen to be you?"

"Yes, that's me."

"Ok. This is about your son and daughter's murder case. Can I come in?" Ebony asked and the woman let her into the house. They both took seats on the sofa.

"So what's going on now? It's been two years, you know."

"Yes, two years and a mistake." Ebony passed her a stack of papers. "We convicted the wrong guy."

The woman began to read, but was shaking her head in denial.

"How so when he pled guilty? And I'm sure he was the one. I'd know that face anywhere," the woman shot back.

"Ma'am, Charles McCants is mentally retarded. There are all his papers since birth, plus his history of doing such things as owning up to crimes that happened in another state," Ebony lied. She had fake paperwork and all.

"I don't see how—"

"The good thing is that we got the right one already in custody." She gave the lady a picture of Gangsta. The lady looked at it hard. She remembered his face, she had seen him before, and Ebony noticed the recognition, so she continued to press the woman until she agreed to talk with Kash's lawyer and write another statement.

Ebony was elated that the lady didn't put up a fight. She left there and went to visit Kash's lawyer. She shared the good news and was told Kash was back in county. The news made her happy as she left the lawyer's office and headed to Grady.

Chapter 21

Ne-Ne

It was a sad day for them all as they watched the news, constantly seeing Gangsta's face, wanted dead or alive, which scared Ne-Ne to the point she cried. The newscast painted him as a monster, labeled him the one who was doing all the murdering that happened in Atlanta. They talked about his first murder charge and his violent juvenile record. Ne-Ne was surprised to hear that most of Gangsta's crimes were murder growing up and that he always somehow beat them. She knew he was street, but only thought he was the typical dope boy from the hood. She really didn't know Gangsta had it in him to do what he did last night and get away. Ne-Ne saw Gangsta as being humble and too calm to pull such a stunt off. Terry even told her stories of Gangsta growing up in the hood that shocked her to learn. Overall, though, when people talked about Gangsta, they talked about how real he was, how laid back and player he was, no flaws.

Ne-Ne and Terry had become close through spending time with each other. Ne-Ne helped her cope with the fact that she was pregnant with Zay's baby and the decision to keep the baby rather than abort it. Terry wasn't a bad person after all. She was just a pretty girl out of the hood who spoke her mind.

This morning they all sat in the hospital room visiting Junior. Mrs. Jackson was holding Keshana, looking at the news. Terry was laid out on the small loveseat inside the room while Ne-Ne stood at the window, looking out at the highway. She wondered if Gangsta was in one of the many cars that passed by, leaving town, leaving for good. She hoped and prayed that he was safe. His phone was off, so she couldn't get in touch with him to tell him to be careful. Ne-Ne knew he wouldn't come around because he was wanted by everyone and their mother. Gangsta had to leave town, one way or the other.

Ne-Ne removed herself from the window. She looked over at her son, her only child. He looked so hurt, so helpless. She was hurt herself. Too much was going on, and it was becoming overwhelming. She wasn't built for this type of life and drama and asked God to fix it every time she went into prayer. Ne-Ne was ready to go back to her simple life.

On the floor under Junior's bed, Ne-Ne saw a blue and green Nike gym bag. She looked over to Mrs. Jackson, then to Terry before asking, "Who brought this bag in here?" Ne-Ne pointed.

"Not me," Terry added.

"Me either. Maybe the doctor," Gangsta's mother said. Ne-Ne walked closer.

"Don't look like no doctor bag to me," said Ne-Ne, pulling it from under the bed. It was heavy. Ne-Ne stood upright, the bag at her feet. *What is inside the bag,* she wondered.

By now Terry was standing next to her. Ne-Ne bent down and unzipped the bag to find it filled with money bundles.

"What is it?" Mrs. Jackson asked.

"Money," Terry answered.

"How— Where did this—" Ne-Ne was baffled. She walked to the door, opened it, and asked the two Mexicans if they knew about the bag. They both said no, which made Ne-Ne think even harder. Gangsta crossed her mind, but she dismissed the thought because Ne-Ne was up here every day during visiting hours, from the time it started until it was over. Plus she did not think for one second Gangsta was crazy enough to sneak into a hospital.

Ne-Ne zipped the bag back up and put it back. *Who in the hell* was her thought, walking back to the window, completely lost. A bunch of people showed love, sent gifts, and stopped by to give support, but who would drop this kind of cash, that was the question. Ne-Ne wanted answers.

She walked over to the counter where all of Junior's gifts, balloons, and flowers were neatly stacked. Ne-Ne did a double-take when she noticed Junior's favorite toy — a toy only his father walked around with. Junior wouldn't take the tiny bunny from no one if it wasn't his daddy giving it to him. A happy tear rolled down her face at the thought of Gangsta coming up to see his son. Now she understood what the money was for and what to do with it.

Ne-Ne walked back over to the window to look out, wishing she could just see Gangsta at that moment. She wanted to tell him that she was proud of him, that she loved him, and to share the news with him about their son, because Junior's vitals had increased more since last night, but she couldn't get in touch with him. Nobody could.

Ne-Ne joined Mrs. Jackson at the TV as the news reporter began talking about the case again.

"Well, let me head back to work," Mrs. Jackson said, putting a sleeping Keshana down on the loveseat. "I know my son. He will not let the cops have the privilege of killing him, so y'all two ladies don't worry yourselves. Especially you, Terry. Gary will be ok, alright?" She hugged them both, then added, "Just continue to pray together. God is already making a way. He is working his magic."

Jerry Jackson

Chapter 22

Gangsta

The Next Day

"I don't think it would be in your best interests to admit to all these crimes. I mean, at least not to the one you have beaten already. True enough, the federal government is at your neck, but that's not a good idea," Michael Swinn said to Gangsta when they met up at his office.

"I got this, Swinn. Just do like I asked you. So we will meet back here tomorrow, right?" Gangsta asked.

"Right." The lawyer thought Gangsta had lost his mind, but all he could do was what he was paid to do.

Gangsta was feeling himself. Even though he was all over the news, he didn't even care because he did what he had to do. Now Gangsta had to do like he promised to God. After leaving the lawyer's office, he met up with Loco, who was very mad at him, but Gangsta wasn't hearing it.

"Way, just chill. We still gonna stick to the plan," Gangsta said. He was happy now that Bam was dead. He felt like the world was lifted off his shoulders. He felt lighter, felt whole again, because he knew that his son would make it. God said all a person had to do was believe and it would happen.

"Way, you got every federal agent in Georgia at you. How in the world do you think we can continue as planned? My friend, this is not a game, a switch you turn on and off. You made a deal with my father, way, and now this? I would never have given you the address if I thought you would not try to do it clean. We do clean work, not sloppy, my friend." Loco was mad. He hadn't ever seen him get like this.

"Way, just trust me. I got everything under control," Gangsta assured him.

"How so, my friend? I have a thousand kilos for you. Tell me how a man wanted like yourself can move my product without being caught in the process?" Loco wanted to know.

"I got a team."

"A team?" Loco laughed like it was a joke. "You have disappointed me, my friend."

"Listen, way. You ain't did nothing but showed me love like never before, so I owe you loyalty, and that's what you got. I haven't disappointed you yet 'cause I still got the chance to show good face. Just trust me, way. You know I'm official," Gangsta said, looking Loco directly in the eyes.

"Trust you with 1000 keys, huh?" Loco kinda laughed that *yeah right* laugh.

"Trust me with your life, way. I won't let you down," Gangsta said, then left shortly after Loco gave him the keys to a storage room where the drugs were located. He met up with Monkey at a trap spot on Glennwood, zone six, where Monkey was getting it together, ready for a takeover. Gangsta pulled up in the yard. Monkey was on the porch with a few niggas under him. He got up and walked to the 442. He climbed in and closed the door. They dapped each other.

"What's up, bruh?"

"Here." Gangsta reached in the backseat, grabbed a book bag. He gave it to Monkey.

"What's this, bruh?"

"Your start off. That's four bricks with many more to go, my nigga. So, is this your spot here?" Gangsta asked, looking at the house. He could see it doing numbers once Monkey cranked up.

"I appreciate this, bruh. Hell yeah, this the spot. I'ma lock down," Monkey boasted, looking at the work in the bag.

"I appreciate you, my nigga. You played a big part in this shit, my nigga. And like I promised you, you gon' be straight, shawty," Gangsta said, and he meant those words, because Monkey was the big help after Loco, and Gangsta was a man of his word. All Gangsta wanted now was to see and talk to both his kids' mothers. Everything would be in place after he gave Ebony the keys to give Kash. His lawyer said everything was looking good for all the stuff Gangsta needed him to do, so he was at peace.

The next place Gangsta went to was Lincoln Cemetery to sit with his brother, Cool. Gangsta smoked a box of blunts and drank a bottle of Grey Goose. He sat out there all night, talking Cool's ears off, laughing, crying, and laughing again. He spoke about his son and asked his big brother to watch over him when Junior finally did open his eyes. When Gangsta left the graveyard, it was 7:00 a.m., the sun was peeking, the birds were chirping. He jumped in the 442 and drove straight to his lawyer's office. Ebony was there, also as planned.

"Brother." She hugged Gangsta.

He gave her the keys and whispered in her ear. "Make sure Kash get this." He and his lawyer shook hands when he walked out of the office building.

"You ready?" he asked, and Gangsta smiled.

"Yeah. Just got to make one stop," Gangsta replied. He talked with Ebony another second, then he and his lawyer got into his lawyer's car and left.

Jerry Jackson

Chapter 23

Veedo

When he woke up that morning at breakfast, everybody in the jail was talking about what happened last night. The COs allowed them to turn on the TV so they could follow the manhunt for Gangsta. Veedo was surprised that Gangsta had kidnapped FBI officials, but when Veedo looked closer at the news and pictures they had up, he saw that Bam was dead. He then realized what the reporter was saying. Gangsta kidnapped the Feds who were watching Bam's crib, then went in and killed Bam and his girl. Veedo smiled, because now he could get the case dropped against him. Veedo instantly got happy at knowing he was getting out.

He walked off when a commercial came on. Veedo took a seat on the steps. A minute later, someone yelled his name. He looked around and saw a guy by the red door: a door they could talk through to other inmates in the next pod over. It was how they kicked it or traded food.

Veedo walked down to the door and shook it before putting his ear on it to hear, "Say, Veedo?"

"Yeah?"

"This Pat Man, bruh. You seen the news, right?" Pat Man said through the door.

"Yeah, I see it now," replied Veedo.

"My lawyer said as long as Bam didn't get on the stand, the case would get dropped. So I guess y'all case will get knocked out, too. What is your lawyer talking 'bout?" Pat Man wanted to know.

"Shit, the same thing," he shot back through the door.

"Hell yeah, boy! I hope so, my nigga. I'm not lying," Pat Man said, and they chopped it up the next ten minutes about the situation with Gangsta. They both were happy that he got Bam's snitching-ass out of the picture.

Veedo returned to his cell until after eight, when the phones came on, so he could call his lawyer to make sure it was official that he would be free. Veedo had to get a letter over to Rock to get him to change his statement, or he would pay him to do it. Veedo was willing to do whatever to beat that case. Bam was the biggest problem he had, but now it was Rock, so he wanted to deal with it ASAP.

Later that day, Veedo got a visit from his lawyer with positive news. "The government is about to release every last one of y'all that's on this case."

"For real?" Veedo was excited. It was what he needed to hear.

"Yes. Thing is, they will try to drag it as long as possible, keeping y'all here while paperwork gets processed and all motions are set, so just bare with me on this, ok?"

"Ok, cool. As long as I'm getting out, that's all that matters to me," Veedo replied, smiling a mouthful of gold teeth. He made it to his pod just in time to see Kash going into a cell with some property. At first Veedo thought his eyes were playing tricks on him until Kash walked back out to grab his mat.

"What da fuck?" he said, more to himself than anybody. Then he yelled, "Kash!"

Kash turned at the sound of his name being called. He looked down and locked eyes with Veedo. They both smiled.

"What's up, shawty?" Kash said while Veedo made his way up the stairs. They dapped each other, shoulder-to-shoulder hugged. It was love through Gangsta they showed.

"What da hell you got going on?" Veedo was surprised and happy to see Kash. He noticed scars on Kash's face and neck, scars that weren't there when they first met.

"I hope giving this life sentence back," replied Kash as they walked into the room to chop it up. Veedo was telling him everything that was going on

"You know that boy Bam dead, huh?"

"Oh yeah?"

"Fuck yeah. You must ain't been looking at the news or heard the radio. That boy Gangsta did him last night," Veedo boasted.

"Where is bruh? Is he straight?" Concern was in Kash's voice. He hadn't heard anything at all.

"Man, bruh stunted on them folks last night. Come check the news out. I bet it's on," said Veedo, but Kash had other plans.

"Them phones on, right?" he asked.

"Hell yeah," replied Veedo, and they both walked to the phones.

***

Gangsta

Gangsta and his lawyer pulled up to his aunt's house early that morning. Gangsta was ready to turn himself in, but needed to see his family. When Gangsta walked into the house, his daughter was the first to get up, running to him.

"Daddy!" Her gesture made him smile as he scooped her up into his arms, kissing her pretty face and fat jaw. Terry, Ne-Ne, and his mother also stood. He hugged them one-by-one. His mother cried when they embraced. "Daddy, Nana is sad. Daddy," Keshana said, kissing the side of his face.

"Listen," he addressed the room. "I'm tired, y'all. I'm drained, but I'm happy. I know none of y'all like my decision, but this do not have anything to do with what I feel for y'all. It's between me and God right now—"

"No, baby. No, it gotta be another way." His mother broke down crying again. She had been crying since last night when he called and told her he was turning himself in and admitting to all the murders he committed. The only thing he didn't tell her was the promise he made to God in exchange for his son's life. Gangsta grabbed his mother, pulling her into his embrace.

"She's right, Gary. You smart enough to figure out another way, other than turning yourself in," Ne-Ne added. He looked over to her. He smiled bright, a smile he hadn't worn in a while. He knew she wouldn't understand, either. Nobody understood, and it was ok, because Gangsta knew that this was the right thing to do, the only way God would give him what he wanted.

"Mama, listen. Look at me." Gangsta lifted her tearful face. He cupped her face with both hands. "Ma, I did what I did, and now it's time to pay the price. And it's fine by me. At least I'm at peace. And better yet, I'm safe in a cell versus a casket. I'm not doing this for me. I'm doing it for Junior," Gangsta said.

"Son, I understand. It's just that I tried—"

"Ma, you perfect. You did a great job. Trust me, you raised a champ."

Gangsta turned to Terry and Ne-Ne. "Y'all finna be straight. I got things laid out for y'all already. Y'all just trust me, ok?"

"But Gary—"

"No buts. Look, I know what I'm doing got y'all confused. Hell, I don't want to go to sitting in no jail cell the rest of my life either, but like I said, it's not about me anymore."

Gangsta let his mother go. He went over to Ne-Ne. She looked up to him with teary eyes. He took both her hands. "I love you, Nya."

"I love you too, baby. Don't go."

"Nya, listen. Thank you for being patient with me, for being hard on me, and for believing in me even when you thought you didn't. I want you to know that it was never my intentions for shit to happen like it did. I take full responsibility for everything that happened. I'm sorry I let you down, but trust me when I say that our son will open his eyes one day, and that's my promise to you." Gangsta kissed her forehead as Ne-Ne broke down crying. "Nya, stop that. We gon' be ok, alright?"

He let her go and went to Terry. She was sitting down now with a stressful look on her face. He took a seat next to her. He put one of his hands on her knee and moved it side-to-side. "Thank you for holding me down through this shit, shawty. I got life laid out for you and our daughter, plus your unborn."

Keshana walked over to her mother and father. She stood between them both. "I love y'all, ok? I know when she gets big that you will explain to her what Daddy did was for her brother and that I will always love her." Gangsta kissed his daughter. He felt a light vibration, then heard the faint sound of helicopters. Gangsta stood up and rushed to the window. He peeked out and saw nothing, but looked in the sky and saw two helicopters hovering in the area.

"What's going on, baby?" his mother asked.

Ne-Ne went to another window. "It's the police. Look."

Gangsta joined Ne-Ne at the window and saw at least eight cars coming down the streets. He pulled the gun from his waist. Everyone looked at him like he was crazy when he did.

"No, baby. No." His mother walked over to him.

Gangsta dropped the clip out, then cocked the chamber back, releasing the last bullet. He put the gun on the floor. He picked Keshana up and kissed her some more. Ne-Ne hugged him around the waist and broke down crying as the noise grew louder and closer.

***

FBI Agent Latrisha Williams

When she got the call that Gangsta was spotted and followed to his aunt's house, Agent Williams rounded up a team to take him down.

"This man is armed and dangerous. Let's be careful and swift. We have a child in the home and family members. We will surround the entire perimeter and then the house, giving him no escape route. I will have two helicopters in the air as well," Agent Williams said to her team as they prepared to leave to get Gangsta.

They made it to the location and met up with a SWAT team and snipers, plus regular police were there, but mainly FBI ran the show. There was no way possible he could get away unless he had tunnels built in the ground. All the agents and officers were behind cars for cover. Some officers ran to find good positions as the SWAT team prepared to move in. Snipers were ready to take Gangsta out at the first sign of aggression. Agent Williams took the bullhorn. She stood near the SWAT truck and raised it to her lips.

"Gary! This is the federal government. We know you're inside. We know your family is inside. We don't want anyone else to get hurt. Come out with your hands up," she spoke.

The news crews were pulling up to the scene. The SWAT team started moving in close to the house. She saw the door crack open. Every officer with a gun aimed at the door, even her, as the door slowly opened. Agent Williams saw a figure emerging with his hands up. He had on a business suit. It was Gangsta's lawyer.

"I'm his lawyer," the man yelled.

"Where is Gary?" Agent Williams asked, walking into the streets and holding her gun down by her side.

"He's ready to surrender. He just does not want do be shot down by your snipers," the lawyer said with his hands still raised in the air. FBI Agent William got back on the bullhorn.

"Jackson, you will not be harmed. Just come out with your hands up right now—"

She couldn't finish her statement. The door opened again, and this time it was Gangsta who stepped out with his hand high in the air. He walked out and stood there.

"On the ground! On the ground!" SWAT moved in on him. Gangsta didn't say anything, he just did as told and they took him down roughly, cuffed him up. Two of the SWAT members pulled Gangsta to his feet. The news crews moved in for some good camera shots. Gangsta showed no emotions when he got up. All he could hear was his daughter screaming for him, Ne-Ne calling his name, his mother crying out to the police not to hurt her son. Gangsta was numb. He was happy, but numb as they walked him out of the yard and down to a patrol car. News reporters shot question after question at him, but he said not a word. He was ready for the next chapter in his life. He was now waiting for his miracle to happen.

Gangsta watched his family hug up on the porch. Terry desperately tried to hold Keshana, who was kicking and screaming for her Daddy. He had to close his eyes before it broke him down to see her like she was. That was the hard part for him: his kids. And he knew he broke her heart. He knew that his baby would miss him, but this was a sacrifice he had to make, no matter how hard it was or who was hurt behind it.

Gangsta was glad when the FBI told the officer to take him into custody. He was already being rushed by the media with all the cameras in his face in his family's face. They put him in a car and instantly drove off. He watched the city pass him by as he rode in the backseat. The two officers who escorted him to the county were trying to make small talk, but he didn't respond to them. He just watched the city. He knew he would miss dearly all his friends, and most of all his family. Gangsta could breathe easy now, though. He was clear of all stress. No matter what the courts thought they could or would do to him, he was at peace with God, with himself, and his mind.

Gangsta closed his eyes and smiled at the way he saw Bam shocked to see him. Gangsta knew that God was with him that night, because God knew his heart was on fire, and the only way to put it out was the death of Bam.

When he got to the county jail, more news reporters were there and the jail staff. They started clapping and praising that the man of the hour finally got caught for all the crimes he committed. Gangsta was rushed inside the jail. The officers tossed a coat over his head because there were so many people out with cameras and camcorders trying to get pictures and live footage of Gangsta.

Jerry Jackson

Chapter 24

Gangsta

His lawyer made it to the jail minutes after he arrived and was placed in a tiny room, a room he'd seen so many times before, a place he was use to by now and knew like the back of his hand. Gangsta always beat them at their games, but this time it was different. This time he wasn't putting up no fight, no lies, no time wasting. Mr. Swinn was seated next to Gangsta, his folder out and open with sixteen statements of confessions to every murder he committed. Mr. Swinn still tried to talk him out of it, but Gangsta had his mind made up already, and nobody could change that.

Two FBI agents entered the room, then a white woman came into the room moments after. Everyone took seats and focused on Gangsta, who sat there nonchalant, like he had no care in the world.

"Mr. Jackson has already made statements," Mr. Swinn said before any of the agents could speak

"Excuse me?" Agent Williams spoke, looking baffled at what the lawyer had said.

Mr. Swinn pushed the stack of papers across to her. "We are not here to waste your time, nor my client's. Like I stated, he has admitted in written document and audio that he indeed kidnapped your agents. He pleas guilty to both charges. And if you take a look, those are statement for previous crimes committed. So instead of the questions, lets just do the processing so my client can get a bed where he feels he belongs," Mr. Swinn said while the agents all read the paperwork.

Every now and then one of them would look up to Gangsta like he had gone nuts. It took them a few minutes to go over the papers, then Agent Williams asked, "Why?"

Gangsta just looked at her. She was pretty. She was young. She was the police, and he was done talking. He had done his deeds, now it was time to finish what he started. He would not open his mouth. "Why did you kill Bam? Why was you so eager to take his life?" she asked, but already knew why. Latrisha just wanted to see if Gangsta would say something.

"Like I said, my client is not speaking anymore. Now, can y'all process him in, please?" Mr. Swinn spoke up for Gangsta. He already knew the move. He and Gangsta had discussed it numerous times prior to this day.

Gangsta saw that the FBI agents were getting mad because he wouldn't talk. It was funny to him, though he only laughed on the inside, because on the outside he showed not one sign of emotion.

***

Kash

Kash inhaled the fresh air of freedom into his lungs. The breeze was chilly, and the taste was lovely. Something sweet and misty, something amazing. Just two weeks ago he had a life sentence, serving time on high max. Kash had adapted to the lifestyle of prison: mimicking everything correctly to the master, the ins and outs of how prison rolled. Kash's mental state was of a prisoner who would never see the streets again.

He had made a sacrifice a few years ago to free his best friend of a murder case. Kash did this out of the realness in him and the fact Gangsta was the best one out the two of them to take over a city, and there was no use in both of them going down. Kash had left his kids, his family, and everything he worked so hard for. He did what he felt was best and was fully prepared to never see the streets again.

It was a surprise to Kash when Gangsta made that same sacrifice. It was a beautiful, sad day in all aspects, and all of his respect went to his brother, his best friend, his ace in the hole. Kash exhaled the air held in his lungs. He smiled at his kids as they both rushed to him when he exited Rice Street County Jail. Everyone was there to see his release, especially the news. His mother and father were there. Ebony, his kids' mother, was there. Kash even saw Ne-Ne and Erica from a distance. His kids hugged him tight. News reporters were asking questions as radio hosts and lawyers were trying to give Kash their cards. He made it to his mother and father, and they embraced a moment, then he hugged Ebony. He turned around, seeing Ne-Ne and Erica. He waved them over to join him.

"We'll follow you," Ne-Ne yelled over the growing crowd surrounding Kash and his family. He gave her the thumbs up and got into the ride with Ebony and the kids.

"Christ," Ebony said once inside the car. She cranked up and pulled off. "Put on your seatbelt," she added.

Kash put his seatbelt on. He was a free man. It was like a dream he was afraid to wake up from. If he did open his eyes and was still in a prison cell, Kash would go crazy. Now that he'd tasted freedom, that's all he wanted to eat. It felt so good to be free, to be in so much space, so many opportunities and so much life to live. He had forgotten how it felt, forgotten that he missed that part of life.

"Where we going?" he asked as Ebony drove down Bankhead. He was back on the west side.

"My house. Your mom wants me to cook, and some of your family is there."

"Where is Greg?"

"Honey, me and Greg been quit months ago. We going through divorce now, as we speak," replied Ebony.

"Damn. I thought y'all was soul mates. What happened?"

"Thought me and you was, too, at one time," Ebony slid in.

"Don't start."

"Naw, I'm just saying it's like you chose the streets over your family. I mean, you left at a drop of a dime, Kash. That shit wasn't cool." Ebony was talking about a situation he always tried to get around.

"You chose first, Ebony," Kash said.

"Boy, I was starting a career. You was in the street. You was the one who was supposed to support me instead of leaving."

"Man, you went into the force, shawty, when you know I'm in the streets. And you know this: I don't fuck wit' cops."

"I would never police you, Kash, that's all I'm saying. But you seem to believe different." Ebony sounded hurt. Kash had to fix it quick. The last thing he wanted was drama his first day home.

"I see that now, Ebony. I was young back then. Hell, you way older than me. I was just lost then," Kash tried to shed some light on the situation.

"I hope you do," Ebony replied.

When they finally made it to the house, there were more people there waiting to show him love. When he arrived, all kinds of love were offered.

He finally got the chance to hug Ne-Ne and Erica. Kash learned from Ne-Ne that Gangsta's son was going through his third surgery. Ne-Ne was happy to tell him that after Junior's second surgery he came off life support, but was still in a coma. Doctors were calling it a miracle in the making. The news made Kash smile. That was something to look forward to, he thought.

Gangsta also took Poonie's charges to free him, and he was also there with his babymama, Nikki. Terry showed her face, pregnant and all. He accepted all the love, but mostly he kicked it with his two kids, because they were who deserved it more.

Ebony pulled Kash to the side after a few hours of him being home. He was in the middle of telling some guys the story of how he got the scars on his face and neck when she pulled him away.

"Come here a minute," Ebony said.

"Hol' up, y'all. Hol' up." Kash was tipsy, she noticed. "What's up?"

"I have a key for you from Gangsta. He told me to make sure you get it. And he left a bag for you, too, but since I see you two more sips from being drunk, I will just hold it 'til you're ready for it," Ebony said, and Kash smiled before turning his drink up.

"Say no mo'." Kash smiled before turning his drink up. Lowering the glass, he looked her up and down.

"What?" She did the same to him.

"Nothing. I'm just looking that's all."

"Oh," she replied before walking off and leaving him to finish his story.

But now Kash had something else on his mind. Instead of entertaining his family and friends, he found a seat in the living room. Unique followed and jumped on his lap. Kash planted a soft kiss in his baby girl's hair and then looked off into space.

Ebony's words had him wondering. His high evaporated instantly and his mind went into overdrive. *What was the key to?* he wondered. What did Gangsta have cooked up? Could the key unlock the door to everything they had worked so hard to attain? Or would the key lead to another bloody summer?

To Be Continued...
The Streets Bleed Murder 3
Coming Soon

<u>Coming Soon From Lock Down Publications</u>

RESTRAINING ORDER

By **CA$H & COFFEE**

GANGSTA CITY **II**

By **Teddy Duke**

BLOOD OF A BOSS **III**

By **Askari**

THE KING CARTEL **III**

By **Frank Gresham**

SHE DON'T DESERVE THE DICK

SILVER PLATTER HOE **III**

By **Reds Johnson**

THESE NIGGAS AIN'T LOYAL **III**

By **Nikki Tee**

BROOKLYN ON LOCK **III**

By **Sonovia Alexander**

THE STREETS BLEED MURDER **III**

By **Jerry Jackson**

CONFESSIONS OF A DOPEMAN'S DAUGHTER **III**

By **Rasstrina**

NEVER LOVE AGAIN **II**

WHAT ABOUT US **II**

By **Kim Kaye**

A DANGEROUS LOVE **VII**

By **J Peach**

A GANGSTER'S REVENGE **II**

By **Aryanna**

GIVE ME THE REASON

By **Coco Amoure**

Available Now

LOVE KNOWS NO BOUNDARIES **I II & III**

By **Coffee**

SILVER PLATTER HOE **I & II**

HONEY DIPP **I & II**

CLOSED LEGS DON'T GET FED **I & II**

A BITCH NAMED KARMA

By **Reds Johnson**

A DANGEROUS LOVE **I, II, III, IV, V, VI**

By **J Peach**

CUM FOR ME

An **LDP Erotica Collaboration**

A GANGSTER'S REVENGE

By **Aryanna**

WHAT ABOUT US

NEVER LOVE AGAIN

By **Kim Kaye**

THE KING CARTEL **I & II**

By **Frank Gresham**

BLOOD OF A BOSS **I & II**

By **Askari**

THE DEVIL WEARS TIMBS **I, II & III**

BURY ME A G **I II & III**

By **Tranay Adams**

Jerry Jackson

THESE NIGGAS AIN'T LOYAL **I & II**

By **Nikki Tee**

THE STREETS BLEED MURDER

By **Jerry Jackson**

DIRTY LICKS

By **Peter Mack**

THE ULTIMATE BETRAYAL

By **Phoenix**

BROOKLYN ON LOCK **I & II**

By **Sonovia Alexander**

SLEEPING IN HEAVEN, WAKING IN HELL **I, II & III**

By **Forever Redd**

DON'T FU#K WITH MY HEART **I & II**

By **Linnea**

BOSS'N UP **I & II**

By **Royal Nicole**

LOYALTY IS BLIND

By **Kenneth Chisholm**

BOOKS BY LDP'S CEO, CA$H

TRUST NO MAN

TRUST NO MAN 2

TRUST NO MAN 3

BONDED BY BLOOD

SHORTY GOT A THUG

A DIRTY SOUTH LOVE

THUGS CRY

THUGS CRY 2

TRUST NO BITCH

TRUST NO BITCH 2

TRUST NO BITCH 3

TIL MY CASKET DROPS

Coming Soon

TRUST NO BITCH (KIAM EYEZ' STORY)

THUGS CRY 3

BONDED BY BLOOD 2

RESTRANING ORDER

Jerry Jackson